IT HAPPENED AT Christmas

PRAISE FOR IT HAPPENED AT CHRISTMAS

It Happened at Christmas is a sweet young adult romance full of heart and character. Christen Krumm is a debut author you'll want to watch.

This holiday story is the lovechild of a nostalgic 90s romcom and the perfection of a Hallmark classic. There's no better way to enjoy the holidays ... or anytime of the year really!

A sweet and funny YA twist on a beloved movie.

IT HAPPENED AT CHRISTMAS

CHRISTEN KRUMM

To Mom — I finally did it!!
To Elsie — This one is for you, baby girl.
To Anette — My forever Hallmark Christmas Movie
watching partner

I love y'all!

CHAPTER ONE

IF SHE NEVER SAW ANOTHER piece of Bubblicious bubble gum, it would be too soon.

Murphy Cain flexed her hand before picking up the paint scraper. She'd been hacking at the dried gum on the bathroom wall for over two hours and had hardly made a dent. Why Claire Bentley insisted on creating her own gum wall "just like that one in Seattle" was beyond her. It was disgusting.

Claire Bentley. *The* Iverson Queen "B." Her daddy's money kept her from being expelled from Iverson — well, that and the fact that no one was outing Claire as the orchestrator of this mess. And Headmistress Kingfisher couldn't very well let go of every girl on this floor. Oh, no. Too much money would be lost.

Murphy cringed at the sound of the scraper chipping away two more pieces of the hardened gum, hundreds left staring her down. The mere fact it was multiple girls' saliva and germs stuck to the wall—and probably a few of the boys'—made Murphy's stomach tighten with nausea. The saddest part about it was she wished she was a part of creating it. Because that would mean she was one of the elite. Not the Cinderella of Iverson Hall.

Another chunk of gum landed on the floor. The piece looked fresher than most. She told herself she wouldn't throw up—then she'd have to clean that up too. At least they had found this mountain of gum now, midway through the year, instead of at the end. She wasn't kidding herself. She knew there'd probably be another gum wall up by then. One wall for now was a small bit of relief.

The bathroom door opened with a whisper and then clanged shut. Murphy caught a whiff of expensive perfume. Keeping her head down, she swallowed the groan fighting to get out.

"Oh. It's you." Claire Bentley shot a glare in Murphy's direction, and glided into the bathroom, nose gracefully pointing in the air like she'd stumbled over something unsavory. Claire gave herself a long appreciative glance in the mirror. Long fingers sporting an immaculate manicure fluffed her already, perfectly-poofed hair. She fluttered her eyelashes, thick with extensions. Murphy watched with growing dread as Claire pulled out a tube of lipstick, smearing the stain on her pouted lips. She smacked before leaning over and pressing them to the mirror Murphy had just cleaned.

Claire, with her doey green eyes and her ridiculously long legs, was the envy of every girl in school. And of course, the most popular girl would be exclusive with the school's hottest guy. Tripp Harrington.

Just thinking about him made Murphy's stomach do flip-flops. Every girl at Iverson had a crush on him, and he was wasted—in her humble opinion—on Claire Bentley.

"Hi, Claire." Murphy did her best to sound casual, but wished she could find a hole to hide in.

Tomorrow. Tomorrow, Claire would be gone for three glorious weeks.

Murphy held on to the mantra while Claire rambled on and on about her holiday, and where her parents were "dragging" her. Barf. Murphy wished for the millionth time since meeting Claire that the girl didn't love the sound of her own voice so much.

Claire's gum smacked. "I mean. It's Fiji. How basic can you get?"

Murphy hated the stupid gum wall even more with its creator feet from her. The thoughts were making her cheeks burn with anger. Sitting here on hands and knees, scraping endlessly. Humiliating.

Murphy would have loved to be out of Iverson for the holiday season.

Growing up it was only Murphy and her dad. Thick as thieves and completely inseparable, they'd covered almost an entire wall of their tiny apartment with a huge map. Spending hours at the library during rainy, New England Saturdays, they charted their hopeful course across the globe and dreamt of all the adventures they'd have while traveling.

Not anymore. Now she and Iverson were inseparable— whether she wanted it that way or not.

"Well, don't you think so?" Apparently, there had been a question somewhere in Claire's monologue.

Murphy sat back on her heels, her knees numb from the hard tile floor, hating that she even felt like she had to have a conversation with Claire. "What?"

Taking a compact out of her bag, Claire pursed her lips before giving Murphy a look of disapproval as she patted at a non-existent blemish on her face.

Murphy turned back to the gum with a roll of her eyes,

knowing Claire wouldn't see. She hated that her courage came from knowing she could hide her expression from Claire. With a wall of mirrors in front of her, Claire would be too busy staring at her own perfection.

"Never mind. I'll just have to deal with it I guess," Claire sniffed.

Murphy heard Claire snap the compact closed and could feel the weight of her stare. Murphy watched from the corner of her eye as Claire slipped her makeup back into her bag with a flourish. She raised a perfectly French-tipped fingernail to touch her protruding bottom lip. She studied Murphy intently.

Murphy forced herself not to squirm.

"Murphy, darling, overalls are cute, but if you ever expect to get a guy to look at you, you should probably put on something a little less ... frumpy," she said with false brightness.

Murphy looked down at her dirt and paint-splattered overalls. Her work clothes. She had two school uniforms and couldn't afford to ruin them. She decided to not to give Claire a reaction. Maybe that'd make her leave.

Claire moved closer, her impossibly high heels click-clacking toward Murphy. She was standing directly over her now.

Murphy scrambled to her feet not wanting to give Claire ground. Not like it mattered. Claire was a good five inches taller than Murphy's five foot two without her ridiculous shoes. She towered endlessly with the added height.

At least Murphy wasn't on her knees now.

She hated that she let Claire make her feel small.

Taking the piece of gum she'd been smacking out of her mouth, Claire reached slowly around Murphy's shoulder, her green eyes never breaking contact with Murphy's. She slowly smooshed the gum into an empty spot that Murphy had just cleared.

"Ciao, darling," Claire said, and with a flip of her hair, she sauntered out of the bathroom.

Murphy threw her scraper at the closed door. She wanted to scream, but no way would she give Claire the satisfaction of hearing her frustration. Hopefully, Murphy wouldn't have to deal with her anymore before she left for Fiji.

Turning, Murphy looked at herself in the wall of mirrors. Her dark, coarse hair was pulled back into a low pony. Her skin, always the shade of a deep tan, was smooth. She could thank her father's heritage for her darker color. Her nose was sprinkled with freckles, a gift from her fair mother. She thought at the age of seven she could scrub them off but found that to be a fruitless effort.

Her hands were cracked from scrubbing pots and pans the night before. She was slim which meant her hand-me-down overalls fit her loosely, but frumpy?

Murphy stomped her foot, frustrated. Upset she'd given even a small moment to the worry. She couldn't afford to give thought to Claire's words when they were so flippantly used.

She turned back to the lumpy wall. It wasn't going to de-gum itself.

———

AFTER SPENDING the rest of her day scraping gum, Murphy made a pact with herself, promising to keep an eye on the wall in the coming months. Gum was sure to start appearing out of nowhere again in January when everyone came back from the holiday break.

Stopping by the refrigerator, she grabbed the sandwich Mrs. Potts made for her earlier. Swiping a bag of chips from the pantry and a bottle of Dr. Pepper she retired to her closet of a room off the kitchen.

Murphy pushed the door closed with her hip. A wave of relief washed over her seeing her best friend's legs dangling from her loft bed. Setting her dinner on the desk, she clamored up next to Emmaline. Leaning over, she grabbed her plate, and plopped down so hungry she'd eat before she took a shower.

Murphy bumped her shoulder against Emmaline. "Hiding again?"

Emmaline looked over the People magazine she was reading. "Yes. Adrienne has invited Jack over to say goodbye and I really didn't feel like watching them suck face." She stole a chip out of the bag and popped it in her mouth.

Murphy shook her head, crunching off a bite of pickle. "How they get away with that is beyond me. Not that Headmistress Kingfisher would be any more pleased to find her star pupil visiting the staff."

"Oh, shut it. You are not staff. You're also a student."

Once upon a time, she had lived on the sixth floor with the elite of Iverson, had even been friends with Claire, but when Murphy's grandmother died everything changed. No other relatives stepped forward and, per her grandmother's will, Murphy became a ward of the school.

To preserve the little money she had left in her account, Murphy was given a room barely bigger than the pantry and allowed to stay on at Iverson only if she worked her way through. So, it was classes and homework from seven a.m. until four p.m., rubber gloves and nasty toilets until she was done with the Headmistress' extensive checklists. That left homework shoved into the hours before sleep trapped her tired body.

Finishing her simple dinner, Murphy dropped the paper plate in the trash can next to her desk. There wasn't much fluff decorating her room. The deep windowsill doubled as her bookcase for the few books she owned. Other than a potted succulent, the only decoration was a large yellowing world map covering the wall over her bed. Red, blue, and green push tacks still marked the various places she and her father had promised to travel to one day.

"True, but still, you are a paying student in staff quarters," Murphy pointed out. "You just better be glad Mrs. Potts likes me. Be right back, I'm going to wash the stench of Claire and her gum wall off me."

Murphy bent to her dresser which, due to space restrictions, was housed beneath the loft bed. Leaving Emmaline to thumb through her magazine, she took a quick shower relishing the hot water.

"So I bumped into The Queen today." Murphy stepped out the bathroom, towel drying her hair while relaying the entire conversation to Emmaline. "She was complaining about having to spend Christmas in Fiji."

Emmaline rolled her eyes. "Oh, my sweet goodness. The nerve of that ... ugh. Cousin or not, I can't stand her."

Murphy tossed her towel into the hamper. "Remember when we used to all hang out and she was actually nice?"

"Man, those were the days." Emmaline discarded her magazine and picked up graphic novel Murphy had gotten from the school library. "What happened?"

Pulling a pair of socks from her dresser, Murphy leaned against the desk to tug them on. What had happened? She tried to remember a specific event that deemed them enemies but couldn't think of anything concrete. The only thing that stuck out was Murphy's move to the downstairs.

"I don't think Claire was comfortable being friend with someone in my 'lowly position'," Murphy air quoted. "She's threatened by my toilet scrubbing abilities."

"Murph..." Emmaline hated Murphy's self-deprecating talk.

She shrugged. "Eh, she's probably just hungry. Too skinny," she joked.

Emmaline fell into a fit of laughter. "That's the truth!"

The girls' giggles were interrupted by a knock at the door and Mrs. Potts stuck her head in. Her apron was still tied around her round waist keeping her daily uniform of jeans and sweater clean.

"Hello, girls." Gray curls bounced on her head as she nodded a greeting to Emmaline who peeked around the wall. "Murphy, I was just on my way out, but was wondering if you could possibly go with Mr. Gruber on the bus to drop the students at the train station tomorrow? Beth was supposed to help out, but she got called home earlier than she expected."

The one reprieve to student working was Murphy answered directly to Mrs. Potts — Iverson's head cook and housekeeper. After Murphy's change of luck, and she'd ended up as her right-hand woman. Thankfully, Mrs. Potts happily took her under her wing and through the years they ended up having more of a grandmother/granddaughter relationship.

"Yes, Ma'am, I can go tomorrow." *Sure* Beth had gotten called home early. Murphy bit her bottom lip to keep from smiling. She bet Beth leaving early had more to do with Floyd and Lloyd Taylor's pranks earlier that morning. The twins, Murphy's only friends other than Emmaline, had switched the saltshakers out with sugar and had tied pop caps to the pantry door. The sugar and salt mix up caused an outburst from Claire who humiliated Beth in front of the other students. Then, when she walked into the pantry to fix the issue, the pop caps scared her badly from what Murphy had heard. She'd forgotten that the part time help wasn't used to the brothers' daily pranks.

At least if she helped Mr. Gruber, she'd be getting off campus for a little bit. They would probably pop into Bob and Ellie's for lunch. The groundskeeper enjoyed the diner's juicy hamburgers on his town runs, and Murphy's mouth water at the thought of their fries and strawberry shakes.

"Thank you, dear. Emmaline, are you all packed and ready to go?"

"Ready as I'll ever be."

"In case I don't see you in the morning, you have a nice holiday with your family, and we'll see you when you get back," Mrs. Potts said a kind smile lighting her wrinkled features.

"You too, Mrs. Potts. As crazy as it sounds, I always miss this place when I'm gone."

"Not crazy at all, dear." Mrs. Potts took a watch from one of her apron's pockets and stifled a yawn. "Murphy, Mr. Gruber would like to leave at 7 a.m., so if you can help me remind him in the morning, that would be great."

Murphy chuckled. Writing it down or not, Mr. Gruber was forever forgetting his itinerary. He always shrugged it off as old age, which left it to her and Mrs. Potts to make sure he got to his destinations on time.

"You bet, Mrs. Potts."

"Good night, girls." Mrs. Potts let the door click behind her.

"I wish there was a way you could come to Paris with me," Emmaline said after Mrs. Potts had left. "Are you sure there's no way possible that you can get Headmistress Kingfisher to sign off for you to leave, just this once? It's Christmas!"

"First of all, Mistress Hyde," Murphy snorted at her use of their nickname for the Headmistress. "left yesterday. Second, I'm pretty sure she would rather hang upside down by her toenails on a ceiling fan before signing off to let me leave campus."

Emmaline let out a groan of frustration. "Why does she hate you so much?"

Murphy shrugged wanting to know the answer just as much as her friend.

"I wish you could sneak away. It's so unfair."

Murphy wished she was the rule breaking type. She could "do it now, ask for forgiveness later," but if she were honest, she couldn't bring herself to buck the system.She only had about eighteen months left (seventeen months, fifteen days, and thirteen hours to be precise) before she graduated and then there would be no one forbidding her from going anywhere.

The end of her time at Iverson was in sight, and it couldn't come soon enough.

CHAPTER TWO

NO SANE PERSON should be forced to get up before the sun.

Murphy's alarm buzzed her awake. Groaning, she pushed the "off" button. Oh, the things she did for a day out —for a day where she didn't feel so much like Cinderella and more like a normal student going in to town. She wiped a string of drool from her chin and tugged her espresso colored hair into a braid.

In order to help Mrs. Potts with the morning chores, not forgetting to check that Mr. Gruber would be ready to go by seven, the early hour was a necessity.

A hiss escaped past Murphy's lips when her feet hit the icy floor. Grabbing the clothes she'd laid out the night before, she dressed quickly. The smell coffee and blueberry pancakes wafting in from the kitchen caused her stomach to growl.

"Good morning, Mrs. Potts," Murphy slumped down on a chair at the oversized farm table the staff used. She looked up at the paned windows sat high up on the walls. They normally let in natural light but this morning they were still dark. It was so early.

"Good morning, dear." Mrs. Potts put a cup of steaming coffee in front of Murphy and turned back to the industrial stove to stack pancakes on a plate.

The back door swung open letting in a blast of cold air and Mr. Gruber stepped in from outside stomping mud off his boots onto the brick floor.

"Good morning, Amos. Get in here and shut that door. You're freezing the living daylights out of us."

Murphy ducked her head to keep from laughing at Mrs. Potts mixed up metaphors.

"Good morning, Carol. Murphy, you ready for this? It's a cold one today and I'm not sure it's going to get much warmer." Mr. Gruber peeled out of his jacket and hung it on a hook by the door. He sat opposite Murphy and Mrs. Potts placed a heaping stack of pancakes in front of him. He clapped his hands together before grabbing his fork and diving in, chasing his bite with a gulp of coffee. "I think I'm going to start defrosting the bus a bit earlier this morning," he said around a mouthful.

As much as Murphy was looking forward to going into town, she was not looking forward to the cold. Why did she have to live somewhere where frost hung in the air six months out of the year? When she graduated, she was moving to the beach — or at least somewhere it didn't dip into freezing temps.

Carrying her empty plate to the sink, Murphy set about helping Mrs. Potts prep the grab-and-go breakfast in the mess hall for the remaining students, most of whom would be leaving on the bus with her and Mr. Gruber. Murphy was just putting out the last carafe of coffee when the first students started stumbling in in various stages of dress. Iverson's strict dress code was lax at the first hint of break.

"Excuse me, could you pass the vanilla bean creamer?"

Murphy's eyes slid closed at the warm voice behind her. She imagined his arms encircling her, kissing her cheek as his breath tickled her ear with a whispered good morning. She would turn and, the creamer forgotten, she'd greet him with a kiss that—

A tap on her shoulder. "Um, excuse me? The creamer?"

Embarrassed, Murphy grabbed the bottle of creamer and spun to face Tripp Harrington. Dressed in dark jeans, loafers, and a blue sweater that only pulled out the blue of his eyes even more, he was the definition of handsome. His hair was that perfect kind of mussed. Like maybe he'd just rolled out of bed, finger combed some gel through it and called it good.

Murphy's elbow bumped the impossibly firm midsection of her crush, the bottle of creamer landing on the floor with a thud. It splashed up on Tripp's jeans and splattered across the floor leaving a white river of sticky goo.

"Waffles!" Murphy grabbed a rag from the table and bent to wipe up the mess.

"Waffles?" Tripp picked up the now empty bottle and handed it to her.

Murphy could feel her face heat. She tucked her chin hoping Tripp couldn't see the bright red blooming on her cheeks. Growing up her dad hated anything resembling a curse word. Waffles was their expletive they used for everything.

"Wait. Don't I know you? Murphy, right?"

"Yeah," Murphy mumbled.

"Aren't you in Dr. Roberts' biology class?"

Murphy's heart was pounding so hard she was sure it was going to beat right out of her chest. She *was* in Dr. Roberts' biology class. She sat at the lab table next to his. "I'm in that class." She confirmed, handing him the rag. When he looked at her quizzically, she pointed to the white creamer splashed on his shoes and soaking into the bottom of his jeans.

Tripp chuckled as he took the rag from her and their fingers brushed. He proceeded with some story about dissecting frogs and their smell, but she didn't really hear him. Her fingers still tingled where they had met his. She was certain she was going to die.

"Sorry again about your creamer," she cut into his story.

He stood back up, handing her the now sticky rag. "It's not that big of a deal."

Murphy's face was on fire.

"Tripp, darling, did you get my coffee?" Claire's honey voice tittered through the air, grating over Murphy's nerves.

Don't come over here. Don't come over here.

"What seems to be the problem?" Each staccatoed heel tap pounding out impending doom. "Oh, it's you. Making messes instead of cleaning them up?" Claire sidled up next to Tripp, threading her arm through his.

"Aww no, babe, it wasn't her fault. I just —"

"Don't take up for Cinderella," Claire practically spit out in a sing song voice. Sweet with a bite.

Murphy ducked her head. Could she melt into the floor now?

"Claire—"

"Come on, Trippy, darling," Claire cut in yanking him away. "I don't really feel like coffee anymore. I think juice will do fine this morning."

Murphy could feel the eyes of all the students in the mess hall as she went back to cleaning the sticky mess. She clenched her jaw refusing to cry and add to her humiliation. Claire would be gone for three weeks, she reminded herself. Three blissful weeks.

Murphy wasn't sure why it was that Claire seemed to hate her so much. She let her mind wander to the future when she would leave Iverson, Claire, and Mistress Hyde behind. It would be her and the open road. No one to tell her what to do or to make her life miserable. She would travel to all the places she and her father pinned on their map, writing about her adventures along the way. One day she hoped to be able to publish a book of the essays along with stories from growing up with her dad, complete with glossy photos, highlighting all the places they had planned on visiting.

"Hey, Murph, you ok?" Emmaline squatted down next to Murphy with a clean rag, helping her mop at the mess on the floor.

Murphy sniffed and wiped at her eyes with the back of her hand. She sat back on her heels. "I'm fine. Thanks, Ems. You'd better let me finish cleaning up the mess, or we'll both end up in trouble."

Emmaline rolled her eyes. "It's officially the beginning of the holiday. I can't get in trouble for helping you clean up a mess. Those rules don't apply today."

"Knowing Mistress Hyde, she'll hear something from her lurking brown nosers and we'll be in trouble — holiday rules or no." Murphy sighed. This was her life.

"Then I'll get Daddy's team of lawyers on it. Because that's just ridiculous." Emmaline's green eyes flashed, helping Murphy clean up the mess.

Murphy didn't care if Emmaline and Claire could easily pass as sisters. That's where the similarities ended. Where Claire was all brash and haughty, Emmaline was kind and unpretentious.

Murphy took the sopping towels to the kitchen and deposited them in the sink. She glanced at her watch relieved to see the bus bell would be sounding in exactly... three ... two ... one ...

The mess hall cleared out, everyone running to either do very last-minute packing or to make sure they didn't miss any important luggage.

Murphy stopped in her room to grab her tattered copy of *The Great Gatsby*. She had already read it seven or maybe eight times—something like that, and the trip to and from town was the perfect time to get ahead on Dr. Suna's winter break assignment. She pulled a wool hat on and grabbed her coat, stuffing her arms in without slowing. Having to clean up the creamer mess had put her behind schedule. She needed to make sure Mr. Gruber didn't need any help so they could get on the road.

As much as she wasn't a fan of the cold, when the New England winter wonderland appeared, she knew it would be beautiful—if it came at all this year. Normally, by this time, they would have had a couple of good snows. This year the weather was just being weird. If it was going to be this cold, there should at least be the white stuff.

Murphy breathed in the icy cold air and let it out slowly. Everything smelled so clean. Or maybe her nose was just so frozen she couldn't pick up any other scents. She tromped over the sidewalk, taking note that Mr. Gruber had already salted the path to where the school's white bus stood waiting.

"Good morning, Mr. G. Need any help?" Murphy shoved her book into her large jacket pocket and picked up a piece of luggage off the roll cart.

"There's my favorite girl. I think I'm good out here." Mr. Gruber took the suitcase from Murphy and threw it in the luggage compartment. "I got your seat ready if you want to get settled. I'll finish this right up, there's only a few left." His smile lit up under his white mustache. "Look, here come the students."

Murphy turned to see a crowd of students coming up the sidewalk. All of them carrying an assortment of pillows, phones, and tablets. A couple of the boys had last minute trash bags full of nearly forgotten items slung over their shoulders.

She climbed in the bus and settled into her spot behind the driver. She smiled to herself when she saw the quilt Mr. Gruber had laid on her seat. He knew she ran cold. Even with the bus's heater at full blast, it still couldn't quite knock the chill from the New England air.

Students climbed in one after another claiming seats. Emmaline slid into the seat across from Murphy, plopping a large purse next to her so she didn't have to share.

When Claire walked by Tripp wasn't far behind. He was playing a game of catch, tossing a paper ball back and forth with his best friend's Nick and Jude. On her way past, Claire bent to mutter a derogatory statement low enough for only Murphy to hear. Murphy's cheeks burned. She swallowed, grateful that no one else had heard. Murphy sank lower in her seat, burrowing under the quilt. Sticks and stones...

Emmaline reached across the aisle and squeezed

Murphy's arm. "You ok?" she mouthed, obviously not hearing Claire's mutterings. She had an entire 23 days, 3 hours, and 29 minutes give or take, where she would be Claire free — not that she had been counting.

She nodded back at her friend, grossed out when Claire pulled Tripp to a seat far back in the bus a knowing look in her eye. She probably wanted to make out all the way to the train station — as long as they didn't get caught.

The last of the students clambered on and Mr. Gruber followed with his clipboard. He did a head count and roll call before closing the doors, always wanting to be thorough.

The white beast lurched into drive, and they started the ten-minute glorified downhill roll to the train station.

During the trip Mr. Gruber had to get on to two couples for making out and another group who were playing a rowdy game of "Would You Rather?" Murphy, ignoring the loud bus, looked out her window not caring that, after this trip once, you'd seen all there was to Ash Hollow. Murphy loved the rolling hills, thick romantic woods, and large estates. She thought the students were crazy for passing up this beauty, looking for other ways to stay occupied during the drive.

Once they got going, Emmaline scooted across the aisle and climbed under the blanket with Murphy. Mr. Gruber only shot them a warning frown for switching seats while the bus was moving. They spent the rest of the trip sharing a Toblerone bar and making video chat plans for the break.

Emmaline promised she would send postcards too add to Murphy's growing collection tacked on the wall next to her world map. Murphy always fought jealousy mixed with excitement for Emmaline every time her parents pulled her out of school so she could travel with them.

The train station was bubbling with activity. The cold

didn't stop anyone from leaving Ash Hollow to travel into New York City. Mr. Gruber pulled up to the curb and the students disembarked in a slow single file. With Murphy's help, Mr. Gruber unloaded the luggage compartment. Students grabbed their suitcases, Gucci and Louis Vuitton rolling toward the check-in station, until all items were accounted for.

"I'm going to go park in the thirty-minute parking for a rest. You take your time saying goodbyes. Just find me when you're done." Mr. Gruber leaned over and whispered in Murphy's ear. "I'll be in the big white bus." He winked and chuckled at his own joke.

Murphy smiled and jogged with light feet to catch up with Emmaline, careful not to slip on the icy platform that hadn't been salted yet.

Nick, Jude, and Tripp were finding bigger patches of ice and seeing how far they could slide down the platform. Two would wait on the opposite end and pretend to push the other toward the tracks.

"Oh, Nick, Jude, stop it!" Claire squealed. "You're going to push him out on the track and the train's coming!"

Murphy reached Emmaline who rolled her eyes at her cousin's dramatics.

"I'm surprised the station master hasn't come out here and told them to stop. It does seem a little dangerous." While she wasn't about to squeal about it like Claire, Murphy was also a little worried one of them, not just Tripp, would end up breaking something.

She watched Claire push her bottom lip out, eyes filling with tears. Tripp fell into the well-laid trap. "Babe, I'm fine." Tripp raised his arms on either side and pulled Claire into an embrace. She giggled ridiculously when he kissed her.

Murphy's stomach clenched.

CHRISTEN KRUMM

How many times had she dreamed of being in a relationship? Of being in Claire's place. It didn't *have* to be Tripp. Although if Tripp Harrington ditched Claire tomorrow and declared his undying love for Murphy she would totally and completely take him up on it. She wanted to be wanted. She wanted to belong.

She shook her head side to side trying to get the toxic thoughts out of her mind. What was she thinking? She was Murphy Cain. She didn't need anyone, especially not a boy. She was going to graduate from Iverson, with honors, and travel the world. By herself. With no one. No one to tell her what she could or couldn't do. Where she should or shouldn't go. What she should want in life. She didn't need a boy holding her back.

Not needing a man was a truth Murphy believed, but there was more to Tripp than he let on. He was more than just the cute playboy rich kid everyone thought. She liked to think she saw below his surface layer. He was kind to her. While most of the students would rather pretend that Murphy was invisible, Tripp smiled at her in the hall. Made eye contact when he waved hello. Those blue eyes of his always turned Murphy's insides to jelly.

She needed to stop thinking about him. He was only a crush. And that was all he ever could be. She wasn't a part of that crowd.

"Earth to Murphy," Emmaline waved her hand back and forth in front of Murphy's face. "Please tell me you aren't wishing that was you. That's disgusting."

"What? No." Murphy would deny wanting Tripp to her dying days.

"Good, because you went all starry eyed for a minute and you were starting to scare me."

Murphy put her hands deeper into her pockets. She

blew out a breath just so she could watch it dance in front of her face.

"Last call!" The conductor moved through the sea of students shouting a summons for final boarding.

"Well, this is it." Murphy rocked back and forth on the balls of her feet.

"Last chance, Murph. Sure you can't just sneak aboard?" Emmaline pleaded, smiling at her joke, but also wishing it were possible.

"If I leave with you now, Mr. G will sleep the entire holiday away in short term parking. Not to mention I don't have a ticket." Murphy stuffed her hands in her pockets.

"Maybe if you crouch down and hoot, I can pass you off as my owl."

Murphy raised an eyebrow at her friend. "An owl? Really, Em?"

"What? You're small enough." Emmaline shrugged her shoulders. "I'm trying."

"I know you are." Murphy pulled her into a hug.

Emmaline pulled back, mouth pulled down in a frown. "I just hate you having to stay at Iverson all by yourself over the holiday. It's a holiday for crying out loud."

"I know. I'll be fine. I have Mr. G and Mrs. P, and the place isn't a total ghost town. Floyd and Lloyd are staying the entire break this year."

"The Taylor twins don't count. They will literally hide in their room the entire three weeks planning all their pranks for next semester and building video games. Their take-out will permeate the place along with enormous amounts of B.O."

Emmaline was right. But there was nothing she could do. She had to stay at Iverson and continue to work through the holiday. It was the deal. "You'd better hurry. The train is about to leave." Murphy said, pushing her friend forward.

With one more hug and a promise to video call as soon as she got to Paris, Emmaline rushed to board. A warning whistle sounding as she settled into her compartment, waving her goodbyes at Murphy.

Per tradition, Murphy would stay until the train was out of the station.

The engine began pulling away when Murphy saw Tripp jump off the step and onto the platform. For one heartbeat, she thought he was coming toward her. That he'd finally realized Claire wasn't the girl for him. Murphy was. Who cared that they weren't even in the same league? He was going to take her into his arms and kiss her slowly as the train pulled away—steam all around them—just like in the movies.

"Hurry, Tripp, I left it on the bench!" Claire's screechy voice sounded from the window breaking Murphy out of her daydream. She caught a glimpse of Claire posing for a selfie with her two best friends, trusting Tripp to get her bag and be able to get back on the train.

Watching, eyes wide, the moment played out before her. Tripp slipped in the stylishly impractical loafers looking like a doe on ice. Still, he managed to stay vertical. He grabbed the bag and turned to dash back to the train.

That's when Murphy felt the moment shift.

She watched in slow-motion. Tripp hit a piece of ice mid-turn and fell back. His arms flailed. He cried out. He went down.

His head hit a bench with a sickening thunk, sending shards of icy shock through Murphy. She looked from Tripp to the space where Claire sat, still making faces for the camera.

Seriously?

Murphy felt as if all the air on the platform had been sucked away. Tripp still lay on the ground. Was he dazed? He was going to miss his ride. She jumped when the train let out two short whistle blasts, pulling out of the station.

Tripp had missed it. The train was gone.

CHAPTER THREE

TRIPP WASN'T GETTING UP.

When he didn't answer her call, Murphy ran and slid down on her knees, her fear as cold as the ground beneath her. His eyes were closed—waffles and cheese was he dead?

"Tripp?" She reached to shake him. No, that wasn't right. Pulse. She needed to make sure he still had a pulse. She touched his neck gently. It was there, but faint.

"Tripp, wake up."

He had fallen on the back of his head. She should check for a bump. She ran her fingers through his hair. There was a large lump on his skull and her fingers were coated with blood when she pulled her hand away. Her stomach dropped. She was not going to get sick. She steeled her nerves. He *had* to be ok. "Somebody help me!" She screamed over her shoulder. *What do I do? What do I do? Where is the Station Master?* Murphy had never felt so helpless. Should she leave him? Try to go find someone? "Someone call 911!" Owning a phone would be so useful right now.

The Train Master poked his head out of the ticket booth

a cup of coffee halfway to his mouth. When he saw Tripp laying on the ground, and Murphy screaming at him to call an ambulance, he dropped the cup, ceramic shattering on the platform as her jogged toward them, phone already to his ear.

It seemed like forever and only a second before Murphy could hear the sirens. Time was always funny in moments like these.

"Murphy, what happened?" Mr. Gruber had appeared, surprising her. "The sirens woke me," he said, pulling her back as the paramedics and first responders flooded around them.

Murphy wiped at her face, a mix of snot and tears on the back of her coat sleeve. "He jumped off the train to grab a bag and he ... and he ... he ... slipped and hit his head. I didn't know what to do." Her voice raised an octave.

Mr. Gruber pulled Murphy into his side, patting her arm. "There, there, he's going to be ok." He was just saying what anyone would say in this situation. But he couldn't know.

"There's so much blood." Murphy rubbed her hands on her jeans trying to get them clean, shock setting in.

"Come on, honey, we can follow them to the hospital." Mr. Gruber put his arm around Murphy's shoulders and guided her to the bus, while the paramedics loaded Tripp, strapped to a gurney, into the back of the ambulance.

A numb haze settled over Murphy. She hardly felt the lumbering ride as Mr. Gruber did his best to keep the bus as close to the ambulance as speeds could allow. At the hospital she was pointed toward the waiting room by a round, kind-faced nurse. Mr. Gruber disappeared to make the necessary call to Mrs. Potts.

Murphy paced back and forth in front of the orange

plastic seats, not understanding how anyone could actually sit in a waiting room. Back issues of random magazines were spread out on wooden side tables. Artwork in various shades of blues, greens, and oranges decorated the wall, making Murphy's head hurt if she tried to look at it too long. Or maybe that was the terrible florescent lighting.

It wasn't until they were transferred to the third floor that she finally sank into a waiting room chair. Mr. Gruber had finished with his call and sat next to her.

Murphy picked at the blood drying under her nails. She was so scared. No person should have to experience fear this deep. She rested her hands on her knees trying to keep them from bouncing.

Nurses came and went. No one had news or updates on Tripp's condition. Even if they did, Murphy was sure they wouldn't tell her anything. Wasn't there something about not disclosing anything to a non-family member?

Murphy's mind tingled. This was all too familiar. The scents, sounds, views. It didn't matter this hospital wasn't *the* hospital, it was still *a* hospital. Unshed tears stung her eyes. Everything was going to be ok. It wasn't like before...

She drank cup after cup of disgustingly sweet cappuccinos from the complementary machine that was shoved in a corner of the waiting room. A married couple and their daughter sat for a while. Once they were informed their loved one had been moved to a different floor, they got up and left.

Murphy was relieved when Mrs. Potts showed up bringing sandwiches for both her and Mr. Gruber. Murphy picked at one not really hungry while Mrs. P tried and failed to engage her in conversation.

"I think I'll head on back if you have everything

handled here, Carol." Mr. Gruber balled the paper from his sandwich and tossed it into the trash can.

"Why don't you head back with Mr. Gruber, Murphy dear." Mrs. Potts patted her hand.

Murphy felt the panic settle in her chest. Waiting for news at school would be worse than being at the hospital. At least here she felt like she was doing something — even if she was just sitting. Waiting. She frantically shook her head as the bite of sandwich she'd just taken stuck to the roof of her mouth.

Mrs. Potts looked at her quizzically before nodding her head just once. "You're a good friend, Murphy Cain." She turned to Mr. Gruber. "She'll stay with me. The Harringtons are on their way from the city. She can wait and ride back with me."

Stuffing himself back into his heavy coat, Mr. Gruber shuffled down the hallway, and for one brief moment, Murphy was a little disappointed in herself that she chose someone she barely knew over the faithful old man.

Mrs. Potts rambled on about how she had alerted Headmistress Kingfisher about the situation, but instead of coming home, the school matron decided to handle it from whatever European villa she had holed herself away in for the holiday. Mrs. Potts seemed less than pleased with that decision.

"Mrs. Potts, what am I doing here?" Murphy cut off Mrs. Potts. "Maybe I should have just gone with Mr. G." The fact that Tripp's family was on the way to the hospital, and that she would more than likely meet them, made her feel like the cappuccinos were going to come back up.

"Pish posh. You're worried about a fellow student. There's no shame in waiting for news." Mrs. Potts said while absentmindedly flipping through an old copy of

Better Homes and Gardens. "Besides, I'm grateful for the company."

When Mrs. Potts stepped away for the umpteenth time to take a call, Murphy decided she was sick of sitting and let her feet take her where they may. Sometimes being ordinarily invisible had its perks.

Through hearing bits of gossip from the nurses, and what little information Mrs. Potts was able to give, Murphy could gather Tripp was still unconscious, but stable. At this point doctors deemed him comatose but they were hopeful his condition would improve.

Glancing up, Murphy realized she had wandered to the patient area. A paper sign announced that she had found herself at Tripp's door. How had she gotten passed the nurses station? Her fingers grazed over the plastic name plate that held his name. She should peek in, see for herself that he was still breathing. She looked both ways. The hallway was surprisingly empty.

What in the world are you doing, Murphy Cain? This is crazy.

Ignoring herself, she took a deep breath and pushed her way into the room. The knowledge Tripp's family would be arriving any minute, or that she could be discovered by a nurse, had Murphy's stomach in knots. Still, she kept moving.

She was just going to see that Tripp was ok for herself, and then leave before his family showed up. No problem.

The room was mostly dark except for a small lamp on the table next to Tripp. Memories came flooding back to Murphy reminding her just how much she hated hospitals.

Tripp laid on the hospital bed, hooked up to machines beeping life into him. He looked so ... small. She had remembering her father looking the same way. It broke her heart. Murphy sucked in her breath. She wasn't expecting it to be so much like before.

She backed against the door, blinking away panic that promised to swallow her if she let it. Squeezing her eyes shut, she bit down on her lip until she tasted the tang of blood. This time was different. It had to be. Honestly, she was surprised that she made it in the hospital this long without freaking out. She clenched and unclenched her hands, breathing to the beat of the beep. She felt hot and cold all at once.

Nope. She couldn't do this. She couldn't stay here another minute.

Murphy flung the door open and rushed out of the room. She made a sharp turn around the corner and slammed into someone. Arms wrapped around her, holding her steady.

"Waffles! I'm so sorry." Murphy pushed hair out of her face and took a step back, tripping on her feet. The stranger's hands shot out again, and hands curled around her elbow, steadying her. She felt her face heat.

The stranger smirked. "Are you okay?" He was tall, way taller than Murphy, with sandy hair that looked as if it had a mind of its own poking in every different direction. And yet it had that on-purpose look to it as well. He stooped down to see Murphy's face. She quickly brushed away any lingering traces of tears.

Pasting a smile on her face she apologized again. "I'm fine. Sorry I bumped into you."

"It's ok. Really. It's a *great* place to bump into people." The stranger chuckled at his own lame joke. He glanced over his shoulder and back to Murphy. His voice was warm with a twinge of a Scottish accent making Murphy's ear perk. "Are you sure you're okay?"

Murphy nodded, staring at the toes of her beat up Converse. She rubbed her hands up and down her arms.

"I'm Hank. Like Tom Hanks, but not as famous and my first name is just Hank, not Tom."

She looked up, bewildered. There was laughter in his blue eyes. Blue eyes that were so familiar. His grin coaxed one from her.

"There's a pretty smile. Let's try that again." He stuck his hand in her direction. "Hi, my name is Hank."

"Murphy Cain." She shook his hand, noticing for the first time what he wore. He was decked out in a tux paired with a new pair of black Converse. "Nice. Um. Shoes," she smirked.

He looked down and bounced on his toes. "What, *these* old things?" He leaned over and whispered conspiratorially. "Don't tell my mother. We were supposed to be going to a business dinner in the city, but then my brother decided to be an idiot and land himself in the hospital."

Murphy felt like the air had been sucked out of the hallway. *Brother decided to be an idiot...*

"Tripp." Murphy whispered.

"Yes. Are you—"

Hank's question was drowned out by the blood pounding in her ears. If Hank was Tripp's brother that meant his family had arrived. She wasn't supposed to meet his family before Tripp could officially introduce her. Like *that* was ever going to actually happen.

As if the realization conjured them out of thin air, the elevators whooshed open. A woman in a long, dark blue dress, nose upturned, stepped out first. She was followed by a young girl in a black sequined dress who looked like she was about to burst into tears and a man dressed in a tux who looked like an older version of Tripp.

"I demand to know where they are holding my son."

Several worried nurses looked in their direction. Two of the three grabbed clipboards and disappeared down the hall.

Hank's eyes slid closed, and he pinched the bridge of his nose. "And they have arrived." He spun on his very new Converse shoe. "Mother, this a hospital, not the county jail." Hank gave the abandoned nurse a smile that begged forgiveness.

This was the perfect time for Murphy to disappear into the background, find Mrs. Potts, and head home. But just then Mrs. Potts rounded the corner and stepped up to greet the Harringtons as they walked toward Tripp's room. She flashed a quick smile to Murphy but continued her heartfelt apologies, no doubt saving face for the school. Murphy did not envy her this moment. Hank took his mother's arm and followed Mrs. Potts down the hall. Tripp's sister shifted not far behind, and his father trailed behind, fingers flying over the keypad on his phone.

Murphy needed air

Making her way back through the waiting room, she tugged her coat from the back of a chair and put it on, deciding to wait for Mrs. Potts downstairs, closer to freedom.

Murphy pushed the elevator door button.

"Hey, Cain. Wait up!"

Cain?

Startled, she turned and saw Hank jogging down the hallway toward her.

The elevator's door opened with a ding, and she stuck her hand out to keep it from closing.

"Mrs. Potts told us what you did for Tripp." Hank put

his hands in his pockets and rocked on his feet. "You should have said something."

She chewed on her lip hopping the pain would lessen her focus on her embarrassment. She wasn't used to so much attention. "It really isn't anything more than anyone else would have done."

Hank was shaking his head. "But still Mother and Dad would love to meet you. To thank you. How about tomorrow?"

She really shouldn't. She could say "thanks, but no thanks", step into the elevator and go back to her life at Iverson — cleaning toilets. She didn't want to meet Tripp's family, she didn't need to get involved with them. With the elite of Iverson. But part of her wondered what it could hurt? The twins wouldn't mind running her into town. Maybe Tripp would miraculously wake up by then, and They'd get a chance to talk without an interruption from Claire. Her heart skipped a beat at the thought. She glanced behind Hank down the hallway. She was just in Tripp's room and had to leave because she felt like she was going to pass out. Did she *really* want to have to come back tomorrow and meet his family?

Curiosity killed the cat, Murph. Looking into Hank's sparkling sapphire eyes that made her stomach do flip flops, she ignored her own warning and nodded.

"Great. Brunch is at nine. We can send a car for you. You're at Iverson correct, or are you living off campus for the holiday?"

"I-Iverson." She stammered out. Wait. Brunch? They weren't going to meet at the hospital?

"Perfect. I'll have a car pick you up a little before nine." Hank flashed her another heart-melting as she stepped into the elevator. As the doors were closing she caught his last statement. "We're excited to meet the new girl in Tripp's life."

Murphy's stomach felt as if the elevator had just dropped nine stories instead of a slow three. New girl in Tripp's life? What had she just gotten herself in to?

NOTIFICATION CENTER

4 missed video chats from Emmaline Harris

Message from Floyd Taylor (05:24 PM)

Murph, where you at?

Message from Lloyd Taylor (05:27 PM)

Working on a new game. Need a tester. You in?

CHAPTER FOUR

MURPHY WASN'T sure she had ever been so exhausted in her life. After finally getting home from the hospital, she'd had to scramble to help finish closing down the mess hall for the break. Since Murphy and Mrs. Potts had finished at the hospital well past the time they should have, Beth had been called in to help. She only agreed after being promised the twins wouldn't be allowed anywhere near her.

Murphy didn't mind the work, or the watching out for the tricksters. The mundane tasks helped keep her mind from wandering back to the hospital, Tripp, and the looming brunch.

It was barely nine o'clock and all Murphy wanted to do was sink into her bed and sleep until next Christmas.

Her computer dinged indicating a call coming through. Groaning she propped her tired body up on her elbow and dragged her computer closer.

"Hello?" Murphy muttered more into her pillow than toward the person on the other end of the call.

"Murphy? Is that you?" Emmaline's chipper voice came through overly loud to Murphy.

She rolled to her back pushing her hair back from her face. "Who else would it be, Ems? You called me." She cringed at her tone.

"Excuse me, Oh Queen,'" Emmaline squinted into the computer as if she was trying to get a better look at Murphy. "Oh my sweet goodness, you look awful. Are you okay? I've been trying to reach you for forever by the way."

Murphy clicked on her notifications. Four missed calls, all from Emmaline. She ignored the two messages from Floyd and Lloyd. "Ugh, I'm sorry. It's just been a long day." She flipped to her stomach and, balling up her pillow, propped it under her chin. Looking at the clock she asked, "Isn't it like 3 AM there?"

"I couldn't sleep. Jet lag and all that," Emmaline waved a hand and rolled her eyes. "What I really want to know is what happened at the platform? I saw Tripp slip, but the train was to far to see what happened. I've been watching social all day but no one has posted anything."

Murphy blinked, surprised that it wasn't on any social media sites. Surely she and Emmaline weren't the only ones who saw Tripp fall. Why hadn't Claire, or at very least, Nick or Jude, tried to get a hold of him. "Tripp is currently in a coma at Mercy General." Murphy pointed to the computer screen at the soda her friend was downing. "And I don't think that Diet Coke is helping with your jet lag sleeping problem."

"What?" Em burst out, Diet Coke spewing from her nose. "Murph, spill," she commanded from behind the sweatshirt sleeve currently holding her nose.

"I was standing on the platform, watching the train leave. It was almost out of the station and I was about to head back to the bus, but I saw Tripp jump off."

"You totally thought he was jumping off for you, didn't you?" Emmaline interjected.

"No." Of course she did. A little tiny bit of her had hoped. "Claire was screaming about her Gucci. And Tripp was being her knight and rescuing her." Murphy rolled her eyes.

Emmaline snapped her fingers in front of her camera. "Murphy, focus. What happened to Tripp?"

"He slipped."

"He slipped?" Emmaline's eyebrows rose.

"Yep. He grabbed Claire's bag, turned, and slipped. Hit his head on a bench, or maybe it was just the platform, but he was bleeding. I'm not sure I'll ever get the blood out of my jeans. Mrs. P told me to soak them in cold water." She was rambling and trying desperately to avoid the memory of blood on her hands.

"How did you get his blood on you?"

"I couldn't just leave him there. I had to do something," Murphy shrugged. "I was with him until the paramedics came."

Emmaline took another swig of her drink. "And Claire didn't scream or anything? I mean, when it happened. That seems like the overly dramatic thing she'd do."

"That's the thing. She was so busy on her phone I don't think she saw it happen."

"Which would explain why she told me to 'shove off' when I texted her." Emmaline rolled her eyes. "She has no clue."

Murphy stifled a yawn and fought to keep her eyes open. "Seriously. Didn't she worry when she couldn't get a hold of him? I mean no text or anything? Her leash on him is shorter than that."

"Who knows. My cousin is postal." Emmaline popped

open another can of soda. "So, have you been at the hospital all day?"

"Mostly. Mr. G followed the ambulance, and when he left I waited around with Mrs. P until his family got there."

"Oh my sweet goodness. You met his family? Claire hasn't even met them yet. You're so lucky Mrs. P was there and not Mistress Hyde."

Suddenly Murphy wasn't so tired. The Harringtons. Hank. Brunch. She groaned. "Oh, Ems. I have so screwed myself!"

Her friend barked a laugh. "How did you manage that?"

"The Harringtons somehow, kind of, think I'm the 'new girl in Tripp's life'." Murphy air quoted.

Emmaline reached to pound the volume, a dinging sound ringing through the speakers. "Say what now? I swear you just said something about being the new girl in Tripp's life."

"Well, I mean it doesn't necessarily have to mean girl-friend. It could mean... I don't know." Murphy gave her friend a quick rundown of meeting Hank and his comment at the elevator. "What do you think? The twins think it's hilarious."

"Oh, I definitely think it means girlfriend, and please don't be asking the twins for advice while I'm gone. Their judgement is so impaired," Emmaline picked up her computer and moved to sit on a seat by the window, the background blurring as she moved. "You aren't thinking about going over there tomorrow as his girlfriend, are you?"

Murphy's pause was all the answer Emmaline needed. "Murphy!"

"Why not? It's not any worse than the pranks the twins pull." The excuse sounded lame even to Murphy's ears.

"And I wouldn't be hurting anyone. I'll never see them again. Besides it'd be fun to see how the other side lives."

Emmaline pinned Murphy with a look. "It's not that great."

"They wanted to thank me. For saving Tripp's life. It's just brunch." Murphy said it as if stating it out loud would diffuse the argument. "Plus, it's a chance to get out of Iverson for a day. I'm here all the time. Mrs. P already gave me permission to go."

"If you need a day away, have the twins take you to the movies! This isn't a harmless prank, Murph. You can't escape by lying — to yourself or the Harringtons. I mean I know that Tripp's a little bit of a player, but come on, Murph, you aren't exactly his type. I think they would catch on. And when he wakes up they are going to expect you to be there."

Murphy hid behind her pillows wishing she could hide from the truth of her friend's words and the sting they left in their wake. "They're sending a car for me tomorrow." Her confession was almost a whisper from behind her pillow fort. "I'll tell them the truth as soon as I get there."

"You'd better."

"I will," Murphy promised, ending the call with a pit in her stomach.

Reality was sinking in and Murphy felt sick. Who was she kidding? She wasn't a prankster. It was going to be an awkward morning. *Nice to meet you, but there's been a huge misunderstanding and I'm not actually who you think I am.* Oh, yes, this was going to go over like Claire finding no coffee in the mess hall at breakfast. What had Murphy been thinking agreeing to go to their house? She should have stopped the elevator from closing and told Hank the truth then. Emmaline was right. There were other ways to get away from Iverson. It didn't matter if she just wanted a little taste of what it could be like to be Tripp's girlfriend. To see how the other side lived.

She should have stopped it before it even started. She should have said no. But she hadn't.

Murphy thought through the next day. She'd have to get up early to prep breakfast for the few students staying through the break. She also had to get a head start on the laundry. Mrs. Potts asked that she be home by noon — she probably wouldn't even need that much time. It was just brunch anyway.

Maybe she'd wait until after the meal to tell them. What could that hurt? They were going through all the trouble of putting on brunch for her, and she *had* saved Tripp. She could at least stay and eat. Then she'd tell them.

The icky feeling in her stomach lifted a little at the new plan. Mind made up, she opened her dresser. What would one wear to a brunch with your fake boyfriend's family?

———

MURPHY STOOD on the front step of Iverson, feeling very self-conscious about her current thread bare, oversized coat. In truth, it had been her father's coat, and one of her favorite pieces that she owned. His smell of him had long worn off, but she refused to part with. She tucked her hands inside the too-long sleeves almost feeling like her dad was with her. Looking down the tree-lined lane, she watched for the Harrington car as her breath danced in front of her.

The pavement on the drive, clear of the snow that had yet to fall, looked like a black snake slithering between bare trees. They stood like soldiers guarding either side of the drive, stretching across the front of the school's lawn until meeting with an almost-crumbling rock wall that wound its way around the rest of the grounds. At one point, Murphy was sure those walls had been taller, grander. But now they stood only waist high, their only use to mark the boundaries for Iverson students.

Her toes were starting to freeze. This was such a bad idea. There were a thousand and one ways things could go wrong. And Murphy had been up half the night thinking through every ridiculous possibility. They would know as soon as she opened her mouth that she wasn't the prim and proper girl they expected. She always said the wrong thing and was forever putting her foot in her mouth. Murphy wrapped her arms around her middle. She hadn't been able to stomach anything more than a cup of black coffee for breakfast.

It was inching toward nine. Hank had said a little before nine, but what did that even mean? Murphy knew the Harrington House was in Ash Hollow, although she presumed it would be one of the estates further out that bordered the town limits since Tripp was a full-time boarder. She was about to go back inside. Her hands were numb, and she couldn't feel her nose. *Maybe* Tripp had woken up sometime last night and the Harringtons had forgotten about brunch. Oh please, *please* let them have forgotten. Murphy had almost persuaded herself to abandon waiting when a black Land Rover growled its way up the drive, Hank behind the wheel.

Murphy blinked. Hank. Hank was picking her up? When he had said they'd send a car around, she never expected that he would be the one in the car picking her up. Didn't their level of wealth warrant them to drivers?

"Good morning! So sorry I'm late," Hank sing-songed as he jogged around the front of the car to open the passenger side door. He had on dark jeans and a pullover sweater layered over a plaid button up. His hair was just as mused as the night before. Murphy felt her nerves go into overtime when he flashed her his perfect smile and did a pretend bow.

The last step was icier than Murphy expected, and she slipped forward.

Hank reached out, grabbing her elbow he steadied her. "Whoa, there. You okay?"

"Other than feeling like an idiot, yep." Murphy could feel her skin growing hot. Why was she so clumsy whenever he was around? She steadied herself on the car door, sliding into the warm car. Seat warmers. Oh, the luxury.

Maybe I should just tell him now. Before Brunch. Did she really want to put herself through the awkwardness of eating with people who thought she was someone else?

"So, hey." Hank slid back into the car, popping the radio on.

"You didn't have to come pick me up. I thought you would just send a driver—"

"Nonsense," Hank batted away her concern. "You're Tripp's girlfriend. Which, in my book, basically makes you family."

Murphy's mouth went dry. "Yeah, about that—," Murphy tried.

"Oh! This is the best song!" Hank turned up the radio, cutting off Murphy's admission, a smile lighting his face.

Murphy watched as he kept a beat on the steering wheel. She'd tell him after this song. Hank's unabashed joy made her blink in shock. Tripp was nowhere near this happy. *Or maybe he is. It's not like you really know him.* She reminded herself.

"Come on! Sing with me!"

Murphy shook her head, clamping her lips shut. *He's got to be kidding.*

"Nope, you gotta." Hank shook his head right back, blue eyes twinkling. "Come on. Your part is coming up."

"No, I can't sing. Seriously. I sound like a coyote stuck in a trash compactor."

Hank threw his head back and let out the deepest, loudest laugh Murphy had ever heard — and that was saying something. Her best friend *was* Emmaline Harris, and her laugh could be heard across the green.

"Here it is. Here it is. This is all you, Cain!"

The excitement in his request was contagious and, without warning, she found herself belting out the song. How was she singing in front of a complete stranger? She didn't even sing karaoke with Emmaline on spirit days at school. How did she even know the words to this song? Regardless, Murphy sang the duet until the very last note.

Hank slammed on the breaks in the middle of the deserted road and turned to look at her. Pure amazement shone on his face. Murphy wanted to crawl into her coat and never come out. Why had she sung?

"Miss Cain," he said in a very fake southern accent. "Never say you sound like a coyote in a trash compactor. My dear, that was the most beautiful dying coyote I ever did hear."

Before she could stop it, a laugh that did resemble that of a coyote shot out. She slapped her hand over her mouth. With one look at Hank, they both burst out laughing.

Murphy felt herself relax. She hadn't known what to expect of a car ride with the wealthy Hank Harrington— maybe awkward silence? But this? There was something so genuinely easy going about Hank. It felt like they went from strangers to best friends over the course of one song. He was so ... different.

"Why did you stop?" Murphy finally gasped out, wiping tears from her eyes. Hank shifted in his seat before turning into a hidden driveway.

"Because we're here."

Murphy's heart sank. "Wait." *Should I tell him now or after? Now or after?* Her brain screamed at her to make a choice.

"What is it?"

Murphy bit her lip. She had every intention of telling the truth but what would it hurt if she pretended, just for a day, to be one of them? She would get a break from Iverson. It'd just be *one* day. No one else would never have to know.

He pulled to a stop. "Come on."

Murphy stepped out of the car, her eyes drawn to the Harrington house rising up like a castle.

"Holy cow. You live here?" Murphy stared open-mouthed.

It was said that a man's house was his castle, but in the Harrington's case, it was literal. The Harrington House put Iverson to shame — or maybe it was the fact the Harrington House wasn't worn. Adorned in Christmas wreaths hanging from the windows—Murphy lost count after twenty-seven— it was downright fairytale-ish.

"Technically, my family lives here. I'm just visiting for the holiday." Hank shrugged his shoulders. "I've actually been away at school in Glasgow since I was eight."

"As in Glasgow, *Scotland*?" Murphy couldn't keep the amazement from her voice. That would explain the accent.

"The one and only."

"That must be all kind of amazing. I'd love to study

43

abroad." She crossed her arms, her breath danced on the cold air.

"You should look into Glasgow. They have great transfer programs." Hank tossed his keys in the air before shoving them in the back pocket of his jeans.

"Maybe one day." Murphy sighed. One day she would travel, it would just have to wait until after graduation.

"No time like the present, Cain." Hank chuckled and offered Murphy his arm. He leaned over conspiratorially. "Don't want you slipping again."

Murphy swatted at him but tucked her hand in the crook of his elbow, ignoring the warmth pooling in her midsection. She looked up, up, up to the high towers of the Harrington Castle — it was no longer the Harrington house in Murphy's mind. It definitely needed to be called what it was. The Harrington Castle probably had a library that could put the Beast's to shame. She couldn't wait to find out. Emmaline was going to die when she told her ...

Murphy silently chided herself. An Iverson elite wouldn't gawk at the size of a house. "How's Tripp doing?"

"About the same." Hank led her up the steps. The impossibly large door opened before they reached the top, cutting off any more questions.

A butler in a three-pieced suit stood inside the door waiting to usher them in. *What?*

Of course, the Harrington castle would be armed with a butler. *Please let his name be Alfred.*

"Jarvis!" Hank clapped a hand on the older man's shoulder. "Meet Murphy Cain. Cain, this here is Jarvis."

"Hello, Ms. Cain. Master Hank." The butler actually bowed a little to her. Bowed! Would he be bowing to her if he knew the truth? If he knew only an hour ago she'd been scrubbing floors on her own castle on the hill.

"Please, just call me Murphy." Murphy shrugged out of her coat and handed it to Jarvis—a far better name for the butler.

"Thank you, Jarvis." Hank handed his coat over, and Jarvis turned to deposit them into the coat closet.

"Here we go, Cain. Into the lion's den." Hank motioned for Murphy to follow him. "Oh, wait, that's the wrong story," he chortled at his own joke.

The door clicked closed behind her. Into the lion's den — if only he knew.

CHAPTER FIVE

HANK USHERED Murphy into a large dining hall, which looked more suited to a dinner party than a brunch with only five people. The table took up the length of the room with enough red velvet tufted chairs for at least thirty guests, another dozen chairs lining the wall. Only five places at the table were set — three of them already occupied by Mr. Harrington, Mrs. Harrington, and the young girl who had been dressed in sequins.

The walls were wood paneled all the way to the vaulted ceilings where two large, circle chandeliers glittered in the sunlight. It took everything she had to keep her mouth from dropping open. Windows spanned the top length of the room, letting in enough natural light so it didn't seem like they were in a cave, but still providing full privacy. Four different flags hung from poles. They didn't look like any country flags Murphy knew. There was one that looked like it might be a family flag. Was it Tripp's family crest? She made a mental note to look them up later.

Under the row of flags and windows perched four moose and two deer heads — one of which sported a Santa hat. Murphy almost laughed, but a quick shake of Hank's head and she held it in. She sank into the chair that Hank held out for her next to the young girl.

"Murphy, my parents, Richard and Tabitha, and my little sister Wheezy." He leaned over and placed a kiss on top of his sister's head before skirting the table and sliding into the seat across from Murphy.

"Hank Harrington," his mother pinned him with a look.

Hank chuckled. "Eloise," he amended. "My sister Eloise."

Taking a cue from Eloise, Murphy placed her napkin in her lap. The patriarch of the family typed away on his phone, lost in his own world. Tabitha cleared her throat and he slipped his phone under the table, fingers still flying over the face. The room fell into uncomfortable silence.

Smells of breakfast drifted into the room causing Murphy's stomach to clench. She was fairly certain, thanks to her nerves, she wasn't going to be able to eat anything — no matter how good it smelled. She hoped her uncertainty wasn't written all over her face. Hank kicked her foot under the table and gave her a reassuring smile. Maybe it was. She smiled back, taking a drink from her coffee.

"I hope you don't mind eating in the banquet hall," Tabitha said. With a lift of her hand, steaming plates appeared in front of the family. "Generally, we'd eat in the breakfast room, but I felt as if today warranted a special exception."

Breakfast room? Banquet hall? Of course there were multiple rooms to eat breakfast. This was too much. "This is perfect, Mrs. Harrington," she barely got out around the lump in her throat.

Murphy turned to the server and thanked him, trying not to blush at the raised eyebrows of Tabitha. Chants of *you don't belong* pounded out in Murphy's head to the beat of her heart.

A patty, which looked like it was actually made of some form of tater tots, was topped with fluffy cream and a thin, pink meat—salmon, Murphy thought. Little black, squishy seeds were sprinkled on top. Murphy was perfectly fine not knowing what they were. She quickly scraped the meat and black goo off to the side of her plate and bit into the tater tot waffle. Amazing.

"Do you not like the salmon and caviar, Murphy?" Tabitha's question came from the other side of the table.

Caviar, so that's what that black stuff was. She was definitely glad she scraped it off. Murphy put her hands in her lap and finished swallowing before answering. "Oh, no, Mrs. Harrington, I'm sure it's great. It's...well... I don't eat meat."

Tabitha looked blankly at Murphy. Eloise continued eating, spooning food into her mouth, head bobbing back and forth between her mother and Murphy. Hank sat back regarding the situation with a silly grin on his face, sipping coffee. Richard finally looked up from his phone. He placed it down beside his plate. "You're a vegetarian?"

"Yes, sir." Murphy chewed on the inside of her lip. Feeling even more so like an outsider. Why did she feel like she could be a part of this world? Even for a couple hours? She was already messing things up. Maybe she should have just eaten the meat. The thought made her want to gag.

Tabitha cocked her head. "I never thought... His last one wasn't...."

Murphy looked to Hank for some help in the matter. He shook his head and winked. So strange.

"We'll get you a new plate," Richard raised his hand.

"Thank you, but really there is no need—" Before

Murphy could make her full protest, her plate disappeared and reappeared sans the meat.

"It's perfectly fine. We were not aware of your preferences. Tripp has a tendency to bring in new girls with different likes. It's hard to keep up with each one's preferences. We know now."

So, now would probably be a good time to bring up the misunderstanding. She picked at her tater tot waffle. Forks clacked against plates as everyone returned to their meals. *Say something.* There was no point in waiting until this meal was over, it was too awkward to stick around. Racking her brain she tried to figure out how in the world to start that conversation. *Hey, Harringtons, it's fine you don't know my preferences. I'm not actually Tripp's girl-friend. Just your friendly Iverson resident Cinderella. Surprise!*

Looking at Tabitha's pinched face, she was sure that confession wouldn't be the best coming right at this moment.

A throat cleared, and Murphy glanced over to see Eloise, eyebrows raised, motioning to Hank with her head toward Tabitha who had abandoned her food and was sipping her coffee. Murphy scrunched her forehead not understanding what Eloise was getting at, but Hank, taking the hint, launched into conversation.

"So, Mother, how are the plans for the Christmas Ball coming? We are still hosting, correct?"

Eloise groaned, putting her head in her hands. Hank raised his shoulders at her.

Tabitha paused, tea cup half-way to her mouth. "Of course we're still hosting. Why ever would we not?"

"I don't know, because my brother is in the hospital," Hank mumbled.

"Do stop mumbling. And Tripp isn't going to be in the hospital for much longer."

Murphy sat up a little straighter in her chair. "Did he wake up?" her stomach felt like it was simultaneously soaring and plummeting. Had he woken up between Hank picking her up that morning and now? What were they still doing here? They should all be at the hospital!

Dabbing at her mouth with her napkin, Tabitha shook her head. "Heavens, no, but I will not have my son up there wasting away." She made it sound like Tripp was in a third world prison. "Especially this time of year."

"You're moving him?" Hank voiced the question Murphy couldn't quite ask. "Where?"

"Here, of course," Richard said from behind his phone, eyes never leaving his screen.

"How is that going to work?" Eloise's small voice asked, as confused by this announcement as Murphy.

"We're prepping the downstairs Oak room downstairs for him. He'll have around the clock access to the best physicians and nurses. Plus, he'll be home for the holidays. Home with his family."

Hank snorted causing his mother to shoot him another pointed look.

"Hank, how was your drive this morning?" Tabitha asked, turning the conversation.

"It was perfect mother," Hank deadpanned around a mouth full of food. "I just drove over to Iverson to pick up Murphy."

Tabitha looked at her son, face conveying her displeasure in his tone. He stared back, chewing pointedly with his mouth open. Murphy had a feeling that may be an ongoing battle between mother and son. She finally broke eye contact and turned to Murphy. "And Murphy, how long have you been at Iverson?"

Swallowing the too hot coffee and trying not to choke, Murphy answered, "Almost seven years."

"Do you get to go home much for the holidays?"

Murphy lost what meager appetite she'd had, and the few bites she had managed turned to cardboard in her stomach. She hated talking about going home for Christmas. After her story came out, they would all look at her with pity. She hated the pity almost as much as she hated not belonging. She wiped her mouth on her napkin and put it on the table next to her plate. Placing her hands into her lap, shoulders squared, she readied herself for the onslaught of questions. "No, I haven't gone home recently." At least that wasn't a lie.

"Oh, that's a shame. I'm sure your mother is disappointed not to have you home for Christmas."

She opened her mouth to answer, but before she could get anything out, Eloise jumped in with questions of her own. "So how long have you known Tripp? Was it love at first sight?"

"Eloise Harrington," Tabitha chided. "We don't need to ask such personal questions."

Eloise shrunk into her chair and picked at the crumbs left on her plate. Murphy snuck her a smile, grateful for her interruption.

A loud, shrill ring from the phone next to Richard's plate pierced the dining hall causing the girls to jump. Richard grabbed his cell, glancing at the screen he looked toward his wife.

"I'm sorry, dear, but I have to take this." Standing, he bent and gave Tabitha a kiss on the crown of her head.

"Murphy, it was a pleasure to meet you. Hello, Mick. Yes, about those shares..." His voice faded has he left the room.

Tabitha Harrington's face went to stone. Not happy at all that her husband had taken a call in the middle of brunch. Murphy was a little embarrassed to admit she was relieved. She'd thank the Harrington's for a wonderful morning, go back home, and that would be that. She wouldn't ever have to see them again. She had gotten her day away from Iverson and had a time playing like she belonged.

Tabitha sniffed. "Yes, well, I suppose I need to get started on the luncheon plans for the Women's Horticulture Society." She took one last drink from her cup. Pushing her chair back, she paused as if realizing her rudeness at dismissing Murphy. "Murphy, dear, I do hope you'll forgive the abruptness of this brunch. We do thank you for every-thing that you've done for Tripp. Perhaps we can have brunch or dinner once Tripp is home. Another day, then? Hank, Eloise, I trust that you will help Murphy find her way home."

"Yes, Ma'am," the Harrington siblings said in unison.

Tabitha nodded, and retreated from the table.

The silence in the dining hall was palpable, but the room had relaxed with the exit of the Harrington parents. Even if the tension in the air had deflated, Murphy felt anything but at ease. She stared at the almost full plate of food in front of her a pang of guilt at wasting not only one plate, but two. Reaching for her coffee, she took a long sip to disguise her feelings of awkwardness.

Hank clapped his hands together, startling Murphy. Coffee splashed on her jeans.

"Right. I think we're done here. Wheezy, mom said to show Cain home—"

"But she didn't say what time exactly," Eloise corrected.

"Yes, yes, this is true." Hank leaned in and motioned for the girls to do the same. "Wheezy, should we introduce Murphy to Mario Kart?"

"Oh, I couldn't—" Murphy started.

Hank waved off her protesting. "Sure you can. Come on, Cain, you scared you can't keep up?"

She narrowed her eyes at Hank's challenge. A game of Mario Kart *did* sound like the perfect way to de-stress, and she still had plenty of time to play a quick game and get back before Mrs. P's curfew. After the game, she'd thank the Harringtons for such a wonderful time, and she'd go home and then not ever think of them again. "Fine. I call Yoshi."

Both Hank and Wheezy stared at Murphy.

She shrugged. "What?"

"You know how to play Mario Kart?" Eloise asked a smile brightening her face.

"Know how to play Mario Kart? Wheezy, I cut my teeth on Mario Kart." Murphy remembered when the twins introduced her to the game, bringing her out of her shell.

Eloise clapped her hands together. "Hank, we are so going to cream you,"

Hank feigned outrage. "I think not, dear sister."

Eloise rolled her eyes.

Murphy pushed back from the table finally feeling there was an element to this world she could feel comfortable in. "Come on, Wheezy, let's show Hank what we girls are made of."

NOTIFICATION CENTER

Message from Eloise Harrington (01:19 PM)

Murphy! (This is Murphy right?) We so showed Hank who

rules the world (GIRLS!) Had so much fun. Can't wait to do it again.

Message from Hank Harrington (04:19 PM)

Yeah. We're going to need a rematch soon. Hope you got your report done.

Message from Hank Harrington (05:22 PM)

BTW can I get you phone number?

Message from Hank Harrington (08:22 PM)

FYI they moved Tripp to a private room at the hospital. Mom's in full Operation Bring Tripp Home mode.

CHAPTER SIX

SUNDAY. Murphy's one day off to pretend she was like everyone else — not currently living the Cinderella life in a closet off the kitchen. During the school year, Murphy would hole up in the library getting ahead on homework, test play Floyd and Lloyd's latest video game creation or binge on shows with Emmaline—Doctor Who (Murphy's choice) or Grey's Anatomy (Emmaline's choice).

This Sunday, Floyd and Lloyd had to run into town to pick up a new console and sustenance—otherwise known as Red Bull and Funyuns. After divulging her brunch fiasco to the boys and Mrs. Potts at breakfast, Floyd told her they could drop her off at the hospital to visit her boyfriend—not letting her live down the fact that there was someone out there that thought she was dating Tripp Harrington. The twins laughed at the idea, claiming Tripp was *so* not her type. Murphy rolled her eyes. Never having so much as a date, Murphy didn't even know what her type was. The twins could suck eggs.

Going back to the hospital to see Tripp was a terrible idea. Maybe her worst yet. But still she felt the need to see him. Felt bad that he could be there all alone since all his friends were out of town. And maybe a little piece of her thought admitting her lie by omission to someone in a coma was better than never admitting it? Never mind that she promised after the brunch, after her one day of make believe, she'd walk away. She ignored the fact that the more interaction she had with Tripp, in a coma or not, was one step closer to someone finding out—and telling Claire. Despite the fact her logic didn't add up even in her own mind, she hadn't answered any of Emmaline's video chats. She didn't need a lecture. Besides Emmaline should be sleeping at 3 AM, not playing Murphy's Jiminy Cricket.

The truth was, Murphy had had so much fun with Hank and Eloise that she'd forgotten who they thought she was. When they said they wanted to play Mario Kart, she expected awesome game chairs and a giant television not an entire room that looked more like a vintage arcade. They played a couple rounds of Mario Kart before moving to Pac Mac and Galaga. She almost missed her noon curfew and had to make up some lame excuse about needing to be back to work on a report. Hank rushed her home, driving the two point five miles way too fast, but she'd made it.

She lost all track of time and the memory of how they'd laughed and had fun stuck with her. That's what it was like to be around people who didn't know to pity her. Didn't know that she was the ward of Iverson Hall. Didn't know that she scrubbed toilets and scraped gum off the walls for a chance at a good education. And dang it felt good.

After double checking with Hank via messenger to see which room Tripp had been moved to, Murphy decided to catch a ride with the twins into town. What else did she have to do today? She'd convince herself she wasn't scared spitless walking back into a hospital, ignoring the fact that her life was turned on its side seven years ago in one that was all too similar. Being a good friend trumped her fears.

After a good ten minutes of trying to convince the twins that she was just wanting to be a good friend and *not* going because she was playing Tripp's girlfriend, she found herself sandwiched in the back of the twins' beat up Corolla. Candy wrappers, empty Red Bull cans, and pizza boxes that Murphy wasn't even sure were from this year piled on either side of her and covering the floorboards.

It was a miracle that the twins even had a car. Janice, they had lovingly dubbed her. Technically, only seniors were allowed cars — seniors and apparently juniors whose parents made a very convincing case to Mistress Hyde. Murphy was pretty sure the Headmistress wanted a break from the twins whenever she could get it. Which, currently, was only on weekends and holidays — the only approved time any student, junior *or* senior, was allowed to drive anywhere.

Floyd pulled the car up to the curb in front of the hospital. Murphy pushed a hand to her stomach. She could do this.

"Okay. 6'clock. We'll be back to pick you up at 6." Lloyd's said over his shoulder.

"What?" Murphy spluttered out, visions of Tripp waking up and seeing that she could be a good doting girlfriend, vanishing like a popped bubble. That meant she'd be at the hospital for seven hours. She felt her breath tightening. Seven hours? That was a bit much. Maybe she could just visit Tripp for a little bit and then walk down to the bookstore. It was probably only a mile up the road. She'd just have to make sure she was back to the hospital before dark.

Floyd chuckled, looking at his brother, replied. "We

wanted to give you plenty of time with your *boyfriend*, and besides there's that new movie playing at the theater."

"Tripp is not my boyfriend," Murphy reminded them for at least the hundredth time, wishing she hadn't told them to begin with. "And isn't it the original Star Wars playing this week?" Ash Hollow had one theater and it only had one screen and never played any new releases.

Lloyd rolled his eyes. "Whatever you say, Murph. And the original Star Wars was two weeks ago. This week it's The Empire Strikes Back. Keep up. What time do you want to be picked up?"

Murphy tried to think how long she actually wanted to hang out in the hospital. She chewed on her bottom lip. "Maybe..."

"It would be so much easier if you just had a phone!" Floyd mumbled.

"I know. I know." Murphy was beginning to feel like she should probably purchase a cell phone with her next stipend check. Weren't there ones you could pre-pay for minutes? She blew out a breath.

There was loud sighing from the front. "Good grief, woman! We'll pick you up at two, and just skip the movie this week."

Lloyd grunted something noncommittal.

Murphy waited, staring both of them down through the rearview mirror. When she was certain their moanings were finished she confirmed. "Two will be perfect." She wasn't sure what she was going to do for three hours, but it sounded like a good decent visit time.

"And—"

Murphy slapped the back of the seat, holding up a finger, quieting Lloyd. "I promise I'll be on time."

They both grinned at her.

She smiled back and jumped out of the car before any more comments could be made. Standing on the sidewalk she looked up at the building; a weight settled on her chest. She had already given herself numerous pep talks this morning. She shouldn't be feeling the pull of panic. This time was different. People visited friends in the hospital all the time. This was nothing more than that. It was fine. Everything was going to be fine.

She jumped at the sound of a car honking behind her. "Oi, Murphy!"

Looking over her shoulder, Murphy saw Floyd's window rolled down despite the freezing temperature. Lloyd leaned over the seat to yell at her.

"You'd better get up there before your boyfriend gives up waiting on you and picks another girl to suck face with."

Murphy waved them off, shaking her head, as Floyd revved the engine before pulling away and disappearing around the corner.

She turned back to the hospital and squared her shoulders. She wasn't going to give this fear of hospitals, of feeling like she was somewhere she wasn't supposed to be, any more power. It was ridiculous. She pushed through the doors, a welcoming warmth meeting her.

Biting the inside of her cheek, she opted to take the stairs instead of the elevator hoping to burn off the nervous energy pumping through her veins. Tripp was on the third floor, but even going at a snail's pace, she was there in a blink.

The nurses nodded their hellos as she made her way toward Tripp's room. She felt like she should have brought something, flowers or a picture or something, anything to brighten up his room, but when she walked in, she decided that would have been overkill. Flowers covered almost every surface, there was even a row started on the floor under the window. It looked and smelled like a florist shop threw up. So much for needing to brighten up the room.

Listening to the *beep beep* of the machines, Murphy waited for the feeling of panic to wash over her again, but it didn't come. Maybe it was all the pep talks that she had given herself before coming. Maybe it was the fact that this was entirely different from when her father had been in the hospital. For one, her father's room hadn't smelled like a flower bomb had gone off. Or maybe it was the warmth that washed over her when she saw Tripp. Walking over to his bed, she studied him. His coloring was good. She brushed a piece of hair that had fallen over the bandage and into his face. If it wasn't for the bandage and wires it'd look as if he was just taking a nap. She touched his hand. It was cold. Before she could think about what she was doing, she grabbed it between both of hers.

"So, hey." Murphy wasn't sure why she was whispering, but hospitals seemed to demand that type of respect. "It's Murphy. Murphy Cain. From school. I, uh, saw you fall on Thursday, and called for help."

She was answered by silence and the monitors' steady beeps.

Dropping his hand, Murphy found a chair and, after moving a bouquet of roses and baby's breath with a tag reading: *Tripp! Hope you feel better soon. Love, Sue S. Myers and Company*, to the floor, she sat down. Depositing her bag on the floor, she tucked her knees to her chin.

"Your room smells nice." The fact that Tripp was comatose didn't make talking to him any easier. She picked at the raveling on her jeans not sure what to say next. Should she confess that his family thought she was his girlfriend? It wouldn't matter, right? She wasn't planning on seeing them anymore, and he'd be moved from the hospital soon enough. "I'm not sure if you're all caught up on Dr. Suna's reading." Murphy decided to go with delaying the inevitable. He'd never find out anyway. "Probably not since he assigned it right before the break, and I think you skipped that day." She swallowed remembering that Mrs. Wilkson had found Tripp and Claire making out in the stacks during that class period. Mostly she remembered because she couldn't stop thinking what it would be like to skip class to make out with Tripp in the stacks.

Stooping over she dug around in her bag producing *The Great Gatsby,* holding it up like a trophy. "But I brought mine. I could read out loud to you—at least you won't get behind." Dr. Suna had given her a secondhand copy left over from years before. The cover was missing and so many of the pages were dogeared, but still it was one of Murphy's favorites.

Yes, Murphy was pretty sure this was the epitome of lame. However, girlfriend or not, a coma or not, she didn't have anything else to do, and helping a fellow student keep up with homework seemed a good use of time. She cleared her throat. "I've already read this one, a couple times, but I'll start over in case you haven't read it yet." She held the book up a little higher. *"In my younger and more vulnerable years my father gave me ..."*

Murphy loved this book, and she loved sharing it with Tripp. There was something about reading out loud that seemed so intimate. Butterflies bloomed in her midsection. If this were a movie, it would be the part where the hero woke up to see the heroine at his side. He'd declare that he knew she had been his true love all along before —

At a tap on the door, Murphy dropped the book.

The nurse poked her head in the room. "Hi, hon, I just need to take his vitals, and do a quick check."

"Yeah, sure, I'll just," Murphy gathered her bag and dropped book, "wait in the hall." Murphy finished as the door clicked shut behind her.

Now what was she supposed to do? She stood awkwardly under the annoyingly bright fluorescent lights, shifting back and forth. Shifting her bag, she dropped her book back inside. Surely taking Tripp's vitals and giving him a checkup wasn't going to take all that long. She slid her eyes closed and leaned up against the wall waiting for the nurse to finish. Feelings of being somewhere she shouldn't started to wash over her again. She *really* shouldn't be here. What had she been thinking? Tripp wasn't even a friend— no matter how much she wished he was. What if the nurse asked her something personal? Or worse, told his family that she had been coming to see him. She had promised herself she was going to stay away.

Murphy heard Tabitha Harrington before she actually saw her. She was loudly criticizing the drab color of the walls, the basic art, and the brightness of the lights over-head. She turned the corner and stopped when she saw Murphy next to her son's door. Hank and Eloise followed their mother, wincing.

"Oh, hello, dear." Tabitha pulled her gloves off a finger at a time, surprise laced her voice. "We didn't expect to find you here."

Eloise gave a small wave from behind her mother.

Murphy pushed off the wall and waved back. Something had Tabitha worked up, and Murphy wasn't sure she should engage with the testy mama bear.

"Hiya, Cain," Hank said, hands in pockets, smirk on his face.

"'Hiya'? Seriously, Hank? You are supposed to be learning better manners at Glasgow Prep." Tabitha clicked her tongue disapprovingly at her son, who answered her with a smile. "And referring to her by her last name like some barbarian. Honestly."

Hank winked at Murphy before folding into a deep bow. "My sincerest apologizes, Ms. Cain. Would you ever be able to forgive me?"

Eloise giggled and Tabitha rolled her eyes in a silent prayer.

"Have you been here long?" Tabitha asked on a sigh.

Murphy looked at her watch. She had been reading for over an hour. The twins would be back within the hour to pick her up.

"Just a bit," Murphy shrugged a shoulder. "The nurse needed to do a checkup so I'm waiting out here."

"She's doing the checkup alone? Where's the doctor! That's just—" Tabitha pushed into the room, letting the door close behind her, cutting off her response.

Hank let out an audible sigh and threw an arm around Eloise. "Girls, I'm starved. What do you say we scope out the cafeteria?"

"You're always hungry," Eloise bumped her brother with her hip.

Murphy looked over her shoulder at the closed door, Tabitha's voice giving instructions to the nurse. "What about your brother? Didn't you guys want to visit him?"

"He'll be good. I think mother has everything under control." All three turned from the door not able to make out the words Tabitha was saying but definitely hearing the raised pitch. "We'll see him later. I don't think he'll miss us." Hank turned, steering Eloise back toward the elevator.

Murphy stared at the closed door, straining to hear

what was being said on the other side. Her emotions at war. On one side she felt like she should stay and wait for the nurse to be done —visiting Tripp was why she had come. But, memories of the fun she had the day before with the other two Harringtons surfaced. No. She had made a promise to herself. She wasn't supposed to see them again. But still....

"Come on, Cain," he called over his shoulder, ignoring his mother's earlier reprimand. "My treat."

Murphy shifted her bag on her shoulder, decision made, and followed the siblings down the hallway. Eating lunch sounded like a much better plan then waiting around for Tabitha to finish her tirade. Her stomach was starting to growl anyway.

"So, Murphy, have you had a good morning?" Eloise asked pushing the button for the cafeteria.

Murphy shrugged. "Pretty good. I caught a ride this morning from some friends from school, and I've just been hanging out. Doing some reading." She left out the fact that she was reading out loud. "What about you guys?"

"Mother has been impossible this morning," Eloise rolled her eyes. "Trying to make sure everything is just perfect."

"Perfect? For what?"

Eloise exchanged a look with Hank who shrugged his shoulders, head bopping along with the boring elevator music. "Mother is convinced that she's going to bring Tripp home for Christmas."

"She was serious about that?" Murphy had thought the discussion yesterday had just been an idea. A Christmas wish. Surely there were dangers involved in moving a coma patient. But then again if you had an unlimited amount of money, she supposed anything was possible.

"Oh yes. She's been busy with that and preparations for the ball."

"The ball?"

"The annual Christmas ball mother hosts every year," Eloise rolled on the balls of her feet.

Tabitha wanted to bring Tripp home and throw a party? With her son in a coma? Murphy wasn't sure if she was impressed that Tabitha could do it all or horrified at the tenacity of the woman to throw a party when she should be focusing on her family. Not like Murphy had any expertise on the matter.

The elevator doors rolled open and Hank stepped forward to hold them. "You are coming to that, right? Tripp must have told you about it."

Murphy swallowed and moved aside for an older man holding the hand of a pig-tailed toddler sporting a "Big Sister" tee.

"No, he hadn't mentioned it." Not a lie. Tripp had never mentioned anything directly to Murphy about an annual Christmas Ball.

Eloise smacked her forehead. "Our brother is the world's biggest dud."

The elevator dinged letting them know they had reached their destination. Scents of overly cooked vegetables mixed with hospital cleaner and antiseptic filled the elevator when the doors opened. Murphy pushed down feelings the familiar smells sent dancing across her memory.

"Well," Hank chuckled. "The party is a week from Thursday, and I am formally inviting you on behalf of my brother."

"A week from Thursday, but that's *after* Christmas ..."

"The *day* after. Mother decided that hosting after Christmas was easier and didn't put her in competition with the other holiday parties or something like that, but really, you should come."

"Oh, yes, please!" Eloise grabbed her hand. "You will make the party so much better. Normally, it's just a bunch of mother and father's stuffy friends and their stuck up kids. But if you're there it'll be fun. Please say you'll come!"

Murphy was a little taken aback. She'd never had anyone beg her to come to a party. She smiled. Noting that Eloise didn't lump herself in with the stuck up kids that would attend—Murphy loved that about her already. She knew she shouldn't, but the party was the day before her birthday, and it would be fun to do something other than sit around and stare at the Iverson walls. But still, this was a little much. Her brain was telling her no, but looking over at Eloise practically bouncing in her fur lined Uggs she didn't want to say no. "I'll think about it."

Hank winced at Eloise's high-pitched squeal. "Settle down, Wheezy. She said she'd think about it." He ruffled her hair and nodded over a fridge that held drinks. "Why don't you go grab us some drinks?"

Hank and Murphy moved to the cafeteria line filling two trays with French fries, burritos, tater tots, and Jello. Murphy grabbed a pre-made side salad, a safe choice, which earned her a side glance from Hank.

"What?" she asked adding it to her tray.

"I didn't say anything." Hank shrugged handing a fifty to the cashier with a whispered request to pay for the older gentleman in line behind them.

"You totally wanted to," Murphy warmth blooming at the kind gesture. "I really like salads."

Hank shoved his change into his pocket, not bothering to count it. "Whatever you say, Cain. I just figured it was a vegetarian thing."

They joined Eloise at a table for four next to a large picture window overlooking the hospital green. The sun trying to shine through the clouds did nothing to help the dull brown foliage look beautiful. It just looked dead and cold.

Hank held Murphy's salad between two fingers and passed it to her.

She laughed. "It's not going to infect you."

"You never know. Here," He handed her a plate of fried food. "Please have some balance."

Murphy grinned while popping a tater tot in her mouth, showing Hank she could have balance. She glanced at her watch. She couldn't be late for the twins. She was sure they wouldn't abandon her at the hospital, but there was no way she wanted them come in search for her.

"Is your coach about to turn into a pumpkin?" Hank interrupted her thoughts.

Murphy's fork clattered to the table. "Huh?"

Hank speared a fry and pointed it at Murphy. "That was the fifth time in ten minutes that you've looked at your watch. I was just wondering."

Murphy ducked her head. "Oh, no, it's just, my friends are coming back to pick me up, and I didn't want them to have to wait on me."

"Can't you just call them? We'll drop you off at Iverson on our way home." Eloise took a swig from her Dr. Pepper.

Murphy shrugged. "I don't have a phone."

Eloise choked on her drink.

"Say what now?" Hank asked pounded on his sister's back. "You don't have a phone. Like, at all?"

Stuffing a bite of salad in her mouth, Murphy shook her head.

"How do you function?" Eloise asked, mouth hanging open.

"I've never really had a need for one." Murphy grinned at their reactions.

"Cain, you are full of surprises," he turned to Eloise. "Who'd a thunk our brother would get with such an old-fashioned girl."

Eloise dissolved into a fit of giggles.

Murphy ducked her head. She reached over and grabbed a fry off Hank's plate and pelted him with it. It wasn't her fault that she was so "old -fashioned". Besides who said that not having a phone made you old-fashioned? She had a laptop. It was ancient, but still.

Hank let out a low whistle "Seriously. No phone. Next you'll be telling us that you can't drive or know what the internet is."

"I know what the internet is, Genius."

"And driving?" Hank's eyebrows rose with the question.

Murphy didn't say anything. There wasn't anything to say. She had arrived at Iverson four days after her eleventh birthday and had never left. There wasn't really time in her schedule to learn how to drive a car.

"No. Seriously?"

"Seriously." Murphy took a sip of her Dr. Pepper letting the fizz burn her eyes. "I don't have a car, so there didn't really seem like any point in learning."

Hank balled his napkin and tossed it on his plate. "That's is just unacceptable. Wheezy, I think Cain needs to learn how to drive."

Eloise hung on her brother's arm. "Hank, you need to teach her!" She turned to Murphy informing her, "He is the best teacher."

"You know how to drive?" Murphy pointed a finger at

Eloise, her turn to be surprised. She couldn't have been more than thirteen, why would she know how to drive.

"Of course. I taught her last summer. We were bored." Hank leaned over the table. "Don't tell her this, but she's a better driver than I am."

"You guys are crazy," shaking her head at the duo, she checked her watch. Time to go. Murphy only slightly regretted she hadn't thought of making time to say goodbye to Tripp. She'd been distracted again by his siblings, but at least it looked like the "learning to drive" crisis was averted. "As much fun as learning to drive sounds, my ride should be here." Murphy gathered her trash and empty water bottle on the tray, dumping it on her way out.

Hank and Eloise followed her to the hospital entrance. Floyd had parked Janice in the drop off area probably breaking all kind of hospital laws. The automatic doors whooshed open blasting Murphy with a burst of cold air. She turned back to see the Harrington siblings on her heels.

"That's my ride," Murphy thumbed over her shoulder. Both twins were out of the car, staring Hank down like two overprotective brothers. Murphy winced praying they didn't say something she'd regret.

"Oy, Murph, the boyfriend wake up, yet?" Lloyd hollered. "Or is that your new boyfriend there?"

Murphy's eyes slid closed. *Oh, waffles and cheese.* Like that. "I'll see you two later." She waved to Hank and Eloise, ignoring the twins.

Before she could make her getaway, Eloise pulled Murphy into a hug. Hank dragged his eyes from the twins back to the girls. "Don't think this means you're getting out of those driving lessons."

Murphy rolled her eyes. "Right," she gave him two thumbs up as she moved toward Janice doing her best to ignore the butterflies dancing in her stomach at the thought of just maybe seeing Hank again. Wait. No. She was not crushing on Hank. He was just being nice to her because he thought she was his brother's girlfriend. That was all.

She climbed into the back seat and ignored whatever the twins were saying. She leaned her forehead against the cold window watching the brown landscape flash by. Murphy had been in love with Tripp for as long as she could remember, so why was her heart doing flip flops at the thought of spending more time with Hank?

NOTIFICATION CENTER

Message from Emmaline Harris (02:47 PM)

Murph? Are you there? I've been trying to Skype with you since yesterday!

Message from Emmaline Harris (02:49 PM)

How'd the brunch go? What did they say?

Message from Emmaline Harris (07:52 PM)

Murphy? Stop ignoring me. What happened.

Murphy has left the conversation

ONLINE CHAT between Eloise and Murphy

Message from Eloise Harrington (07:53 PM)

You know our dad owns a cell phone company right? We can totally hook you up

Message from Murphy Cain (07:55 PM)

Haha. Thanks, Wheezy, but that's okay. Really. I'm totally fine without one.

Message from Eloise Harrington (07:55 PM)

You are so weird. If you ever change your mind...

CHAPTER SEVEN

LAUNDRY DAY. The day Murphy gathered, washed, dried, folded and returned clothes to their owners. The day she felt most like Cinderella. Washing someone else's clothes was right up there with scraping gum off bathroom walls. The chore seemed worse during the break since so many students opted to have it done before they returned. Everyone wore uniforms. How did they produce so much extra laundry?

Murphy checked her list. Every order had been picked up, save for one (actually, two). The missing laundry? Floyd and Lloyd. Murphy rolled her eyes. It was a good thing they had Murphy in their life or they would never have clean clothes. Which meant they'd most likely just have a new batch delivered every week from Gap or Abercrombie until they were trapped under a mountain of dirty clothes in their bedroom.

Murphy knocked and after hearing the okay to enter, poked her head in the twins' room.

"Hey, guys, I'm here to pick up your laundry." Murphy

blinked against the darkness. "You forgot to leave it in the hall."

The canvas laundry bags were sitting just inside the door — of course they forgot the last step.

"Murphy, come here, you gotta see this!" Floyd called out from inside the cave like room.

"Why do you have it so dark in here?" Murphy flipped the light on ignoring the boys' groans.

Lloyd clapped his hands over his eyes. "Man, we just wanted to show you this first level of our new game. Why'd you have to go and blind us, woman?"

Murphy rolled her eyes. "You seriously need to get some Febreze, guys. It smells like the inside of a Funyuns bag in here."

Both Floyd and Lloyd turned to her with blank stares. "And that's a bad thing?"

"So what did you want to show me?" Murphy shook her head. They were a lost cause.

"This," Floyd jumped out of his computer chair and motioned for Murphy to sit.

Murphy dropped the bags to the floor and sank into the computer chair.

"Okay, so basically, you're that knight there." Floyd pointed to a figure on the screen.

"Sir Siegfried," Lloyd inserted from behind his computer monitor. The boys had pushed their desks together in the middle of the room, so they could face each other. Murphy was surprised she didn't trip over the wires snaked every which way across the floor. "I named him."

Murphy nodded. "Sir Siegfried. Right, so what's the objective?" she asked, hands hovering over the keypad ready to do as instructed.

"The overall objective will be to rescue Princess Buttercup. This is just level one. Each level you will need to collect hidden gems to pay off the trolls and advance to the next level."

Click, click.

Murphy found a gem and had Sir Siegfried pick it up and put in his knapsack. Floyd spluttered as Murphy found four more in quick succession. "It's supposed to be a little bit more challenging than that."

Murphy smiled keeping her focus on the game at hand. She knew how the twins thought. She had this level in the bag.

"We put a surprise obstacle at the end." Floyd bragged, taking a gulp of his Red Bull. "It's ok if it takes you a couple of times to actually get past—"

"Finished," Murphy cut him off as a cheerful theme jingle played announcing the completion of the level. She spun from the desk, smirking at the look of disbelief on Floyd's face. She reached into the bottom drawer and pulled out a handful of the peanut butter M&Ms she knew Floyd kept there for her.

"Say what now?" Floyd pushed her out of the chair and slid in it himself, his nose practically shoved against the screen, typing furiously at the keyboard. "That's impossible."

"Obviously not, Genius," Lloyd shot back, chewing on a Red Vine, nose just as close to his monitor.

Murphy popped the M&Ms in her mouth as she hefted the twin's laundry bag and the other two that she had dropped.

"Hey, Murph," Lloyd called out, not looking away from his screen. "You might want to check on your boyfriend's cat."

"He's not my—"

CHRISTEN KRUMM

"Yeah. Sure," Lloyd mumbled, mind already focus back on his screen. "Still. The cat."

Murphy let the door close behind her. Yes. The cat. Fiona. How could she have forgotten?

Fiona had started out as a dare for Tripp. The whole school knew about the contraband cat. How Headmistress Kingfisher hadn't gotten wind of it — or maybe she had and just chosen to look the other way not wanting to upset her most prized (re: financially beneficial) student. Fiona had been a half-dead stray Tripp and his friends found in town. Jude had bet him twenty bucks that he couldn't smuggle her into the school, and Nick had doubled down that he couldn't keep her alive for a month without getting caught. Almost a year later and Murphy felt like she was part of the conspiracy since she took out a bag of used litter to the trash bin weekly and still hadn't turned him in.

Tripp's room was just down the hall from the twins. Murphy bit her lip, twisting the master key between her fingers. She was pretty sure this wasn't what Mrs. P had in mind when she handed it to Murphy. If she did use it, when Tripp woke up, he'd be so thankful that she had kept Fiona alive. He did love that cat. Besides if she didn't use it things would probably start getting smelly — then he would be found out, and all those months of hiding would be for naught. What had Tripp planned on doing during the break? Now that Murphy knew how close his house was, maybe he had planned on coming back and smuggling her home — or at least making sure she had food and litter changed every few days.

She squeezed the key in her fist. Mind made up, she left the laundry bags in front of the twin's room. Inserting the key in the lock to Tripp's room, she pushed the door open.

74

She gagged when stale air smelling of kitty litter and the lingering scent of Tripp's cologne hit her in the face.

This. This was why she was not an animal fan. The culprit of the horrid stench was nowhere to be found. Murphy silently prayed that she wasn't going to find a dead cat. That would definitely top the gum wall as the most disgusting thing she had to clean up.

She pushed up her sleeves. She could straighten his room up a bit while she was here. Maybe it wouldn't require a cleaning crew when Tripp returned to school. And maybe, just maybe, Murphy would be able to help Tripp keep the secret of Fiona just a little longer.

Once Murphy started moving around the room, Fiona sauntered from under the bed, stretching lazily.

The cat tangled herself around Murphy's ankles. "You hungry, girl?" She knelt to scratch between Fiona's ears. She let out an agitated meow and batted away Murphy's hand.

"Ok, ok, calm down. I'll get your food." Murphy stood, hands on hips, and surveyed the room. Peeking into the closet, she found the empty food bowl and almost empty water bowl. But where was the cat food hidden?

She looked in the wardrobe, the bottom desk drawer, and behind the nightstand. Nothing. She bent over to look under the bed.

"Bingo." Shoved under the bed sandwiched between an empty burger wrapper and a rumpled sweater sat a bag of cat food specialized for indoor kittens, top rolled closed. A little further behind that was a clear plastic box with kitty litter.

Murphy slithered under the bed, stretching her five-foot-two frame as far as it would allow, but her fingers just brushed the bag. This bed was way too big. Curling her toes, she pushed herself further under the bed finally grabbing the bag. She pulled it to herself before reaching to grab the box of litter as well, freeing both from their dark prison.

She crawled out from under the bed relieved there wasn't anyone to witness her very unladylike shimmy. Wiping her hands on the back of her jeans she unrolled the bag making sure it actually was cat food and not just a hiding place for other contraband.

"Hi."

Murphy screamed and the bag of food flew over her head, raining cat food down around her like a perpetual hailstorm. She turned to find Hank leaning against the desk, hands folded across his chest.

"Wh—what are you doing here?" Murphy pulled down her shirt and pushed her hair behind her ear praying that she didn't look as horribly disheveled as she felt.

Hank pushed off the desk and reached over and picked a piece of cat food out of her hair, tossing it to the floor. "I just came over to grab some stuff for Tripp. They are bringing him home tomorrow."

Murphy swiped her hand over her hair, hoping there was no more cat food lodged anywhere (although she was pretty sure there were a couple pieces stuck in her bra). "He woke up?" She asked hopefully.

"Nope," Hank shook his head. "Mother convinced the hospital, with a large donation, to let her continue his care at home."

Fiona, not minding that her food was all over the floor, was currently eating as much as she could, as fast as she could. "Hello, you." Hank bent over and scooped her up. Fiona nipped at him before jumping over his shoulder back to her dinner below. "Okay then."

"That's Fiona. She doesn't really like to be touched." Murphy hefted the litter and carried it to the litter box.

"Apparently." Hank held open the trash bag while Murphy dumped the old litter. "Why is she in Tripp's room? I thought pets were against school policy."

"Totally against school policy. Fiona was a bet, nine months ago." Murphy shook out new litter. "I think Tripp got a little attached to her, and she hasn't left."

"Huh. Of course there would be a bet involved. Still didn't peg my brother for a cat person." Hank tied the bag and placed it by the door.

"I don't think your brother is a cat person. I think he's just a Fiona person." Murphy scooped up as much of the cat food back into the bag as she could. She'd vacuum up the rest later. "Do you want to take her home? He'd probably like having her around."

"Mother would have a cow." Hank replied, amused. "For one, she's convinced a cat would eat her face off when she's sleeping."

"She does have a point." Murphy agreed.

Hank shook his head. "Second of all, she's convinced she's allergic to them." He opened the wardrobe and tossed Tripp's overnight bag onto the bed.

"Is she?" Murphy asked straightening the pillows on Tripp's bed and pulling the covers tight.

"Is she what?" Hank asked sticking his head out of the wardrobe.

"Allergic to cats?" Murphy asked, putting a pile of dirty clothes in the hallway. Might has well get to them, even if he hadn't signed up for the extra laundry service.

"Nah. I think that was just an excuse she made when we kids were growing up and wanted a pet." Hank climbed out of the wardrobe with a pile of rumpled clothes. "Good grief, my brother is a slob."

Murphy chuckled, silently agreeing, as she straightened

the various piles of papers and books on his desk. She was not a fan of slobs. Tripp must have just gotten busy. She made excuses for him in her mind.

Hank folded the clothes and put them in a bag. Murphy added a thick throw to the top. The Harrington's probably had plenty of throws and blankets, but this one looked worn in. It was obviously a favorite. If the roles were reversed, she knew she'd want something familiar. And since taking Fiona was out ...

"Thanks." Hank said zipping the bag and putting the strap over his shoulder. He stepped over Fiona still chowing down on the leftover food. If she kept going, Murphy wouldn't have to worry about bringing the vacuum back up later.

"Well, then." Hank turned to Murphy, thumb looped through the strap across his chest.

Murphy stood, empty pizza boxes and cans of soda from under the bed and in her hands. She felt squirmy under Hank's gaze. Why was he staring at her?

His eyes narrowed. "Why are you cleaning Tripp's room? Aren't there people here that do that?"

Murphy turned to keep Hank from seeing her face turn bright red. She was the "people" that did *that*. Tossing the trash into a can next to his desk, she wiped her hands on the back of her pants. "Yeah, I guess there are." She shrugged. He was so going to see through her.

"Tomorrow then." Hank declared. "I'll pick you up at noon."

"What happens at noon?" Murphy asked. There was no way she had made plans with Hank. She told herself yesterday was the last time she would see him or his family. It wasn't her fault he kept popping up.

Hank grinned at her and bopped his finger on her nose.

"Tomorrow at noon, Murphy Cain, is when you learn how to drive."

———

AFTER HANK LEFT, Murphy had gathered up the rest of the laundry, but couldn't stop thinking about Fiona being alone in Tripp's room. Then again, she might have been thinking about Fiona so that she *didn't* have to think about Hank's stupid declaration that she was going to learn to drive tomorrow. Either way, obsessing over Fiona irked her to no end — especially because they were talking about a cat.

Eventually, Floyd and Lloyd helped her move the contraband kitty, her litter box, food bowl, and random toys down to Murphy's room. She'd move it all back before the students returned for the start of the new semester. If Tripp wasn't back then she'd figure something out before Headmistress Kingfisher returned from her holiday. If Fiona was discovered in her room, Murphy would be expelled for sure.

So far, Fiona had been in her new quarters for a little over two hours and she seemed to love exploring. Murphy was trying to play with her by dangling a puff ball attached to a string over the side of her bed, but Fiona was more interested in jumping from the desk, to the bed, disappearing behind the bed, and doing it all over again.

Ignoring the missed calls notification in the corner of the screen of her computer, Murphy tried to open the music app. Fiona had detoured from her route and pounced on the keypad. Which is how she accidentally answered Emmaline's next call.

"Murphy?"

79

Murphy groaned internally. She shoved Fiona off her computer and pulled her laptop to her. "Hi, Emmaline."

"Please don't tell me that is Fiona the contraband cat." Emmaline had moved closer to the screen as if that would help her see where Fiona had disappeared to. "In your room."

"Okay. I won't." Murphy didn't feel like talking. She wasn't in the mood for the lecture. She already knew everything Emmaline was going to say. Probably nothing Murphy hadn't already told herself.

Emmaline sat back on her bed, her eyes doing that weird intense thing that she normally reserved for Floyd, Lloyd, and their antics. Murphy and Emmaline went together like Bert and Ernie, peanut butter and jelly, pancakes and syrup. They had never had so much as a disagreement before and the silence between them felt like trying to run with wads of gum stuck to the bottom of her shoes.

"Why is the contraband cat in your room?" Emmaline finally broke the silence.

"I felt bad because she was alone in Tripp's room." Fiona finally settled down and curled up on Murphy's lap almost like she was shielding her from the coming onslaught from Emmaline. "And what else was I supposed to do? I didn't really feel like ending up with a dead cat in a month. Because you know I'd be the one that would have to clean *that* up."

"I don't know what you were supposed to do. Anything but this." Emmaline spluttered. "If Mistress Hyde finds out, she'll kick you out!"

Murphy tugged her hair over her shoulder and started braiding it. "She's not going to find out."

"How do you know?" Emmaline crossed her arms.

"She just won't. I'll put her back before the Hyde returns." Murphy held her pinky up to the computer. "Pinky promise."

Emmaline pursed her lips. "Just be careful."

"I am." Murphy dropped her hand and started rubbing in between Fiona's ears. Fiona purred so loudly Murphy's lap was vibrating.

"And stop getting attached." Her friend pointed a finger at the screen in her direction.

When Murphy paused, Fiona jumped off her lap and went back to exploring.

After an uncomfortable silence, Emmaline asked. "Why are you ignoring my calls?"

"I'm not ignoring your calls," Murphy protested.

"I've called four times, and after seeing Fiona and the way you reacted after answering, I'm assuming I owe one to Fiona for being the one to answer my call because you for sure weren't going to picking up." Emmaline raised a pretend glass in the air to toast the cat.

"I haven't been ignoring you on purpose," Murphy shrugged. It had totally been on purpose. The realization stung. "I've just been really busy."

"Your day off was yesterday, Murphy. It's not like you have a ton of friends to hang out with or a bursting schedule." Emmaline winced as she realized what she just said. "Murphy, I'm sorry, I didn't mean—"

Murphy felt like she had been punched in the stomach. "Suck eggs, Emmaline. I was busy yesterday. I went to see Tripp again at the hospital. Just trying to be a good friend, and I bumped into Hank and Eloise and we ended up hanging out." She decided to leave out the fact that she had seen Hank again that morning.

"Who?"

"Tripp's brother and sister."

Emmaline's face brightened. "So, then you *did* tell his family on Saturday you aren't really his girlfriend and they were cool with it."

There it was. The question Murphy had been silently begging Emmaline not to ask. But she knew she would. Which brought her back to why she wasn't answering her calls. Stupid cat. "No. I haven't actually. It didn't come up."

"It didn't come up? Murphy, I can't believe you."

"What does it matter? I wasn't planning on seeing them again, but they just keep popping up."

"So then you tell them!" Emmaline burst out.

"Maybe once Tripp wakes up—"

"Murphy, stop. This isn't the movies. This is real life. Tripp isn't going to wake up and declare his undying love for you." Emmaline slashed into her unfinished fantasy. Sometimes Murphy thought Emmaline knew her too well.

"But it could happen."

Emmaline's eyebrows shot up. "No, Murph, it can't. Besides, you really think Claire will go for that?"

"I don't care about Claire." Her shoulders met her ears in a shrug. Right at this moment she didn't care. She wanted this. Wanted to be part of the in crowd. She wanted the hottest guy in school at her side. Anytime Claire came around, Murphy tried to be the bigger person and walk away, just accept that she wasn't a part of that crowd.

Okay, she hadn't tried that hard to tell the Tripp's family that she wasn't really his girlfriend, but she *had* walked away twice. It wasn't her fault she kept bumping into a Harrington. Maybe it was a sign that the universe wanted them together too. She should just stop fighting it.

Emmaline's eyes shrunk to slits. "What's going on, Murphy. This isn't you. You aren't a conniving liar."

Throwing up her arms, Murphy startled Fiona who shot across the room and hid behind her desk. "What if it is? What if this is the real me? The me Tripp could be with."

"Then I don't think we can be friends."

Murphy sucked in a breath. "Whatever, Emmaline." She slammed her computer shut.

She was done listening. Who cared if she changed a little bit? Like she said, eventually Tripp would wake up, and she would be the one at his side. She could prove that she deserved this life. That she was the girl for him. There was no harm in a little dreaming. Right?

NOTIFICATION CENTER

Message from Floyd Taylor (09:12 PM)

Reworking the game. Should be ready for you in the next couple of days. Don't expect to win so easily next time. *insert evil laugh*

CHAPTER EIGHT

HOW DID Murphy get herself into this mess? Her mouth was bone dry, and she felt like she was about to pee her pants. She rubbed her damp palms against her jeans trying to process what Hank was explaining to her for the second time.

"Clutch, brake, gas." He pointed to the three pedals at the car's floor. "You press the clutch in to change gears. Break and clutch together to stop. Gas to go. Got it?"

Murphy swallowed — or tried to. "I thought there were only two pedals."

"Yeah, that's an automatic. This is a standard. Much more fun to drive." Hank looked into Murphy's panicking eyes. "Hey. You got this. Really. I wouldn't teach you to drive if I didn't have all the faith that you could do it." Hank smacked his hands together and slid out of the driver's seat. "Your turn. Let's go through the gears before we start her up and drive around."

Hank had picked Murphy up at noon sharp — *of course* he had been on time. Thankfully she'd just managed to get just enough done that Mrs. Potts let her have the afternoon off.

The entire drive to the park, Murphy pressed her hands to her knees to keep them from bouncing. The city park was completely abandoned due to the cold, which Murphy found as a small blessing. At least there wouldn't be any kids playing for her to accidentally run over.

Murphy plunked into the driver's seat, white knuckling the steering wheel. Hank opened the passenger side door in a burst of freezing air and slid into the seat. The scent of his cinnamon gum distracted her for half a second.

Chuckling, Hank brushed her knuckles with a finger. "Ease up a bit."

As if she could ease up at all with the tingles shooting up her arm at his touch. Murphy flexed her hand and put it on the gear shift.

"Okay. Before we start her up, let's just practice going through the gears. Put one foot on the break and one on the clutch." Hank turned in his seat, one hand on the dash, the other rested on the back of Murphy's seat. He exuded confidence and always looked like he was ready to laugh at a joke or hold you while you cried.

Murphy swallowed. Why was she thinking about Hank holding her while she cried? Taking a deep breath, she pressed in the break and clutch.

"Ok. You're in neutral, so move to first gear."

She froze. Where was first gear?

Hank slid his hand over hers. "Here." He pushed the stick up and over.

Murphy's brain froze, not able to comprehend anything Hank was saying. She stared down at their hands resting on the gear shift.

"Got it? Your turn." Hank moved his hand back to the dash, breaking Murphy out of her trance.

She forced herself to move. First gear. Up and over. Second. Straight down and so on until she brought it back to rest in neutral.

"Great. Now move to second again."

Hank had her move through the gears a couple more times before announcing it was time to start the car. He explained how, in order to move the car, she was going to have to feather between the clutch and the gas.

Despite her hurting brain, Murphy thought she understood the general idea of what she was supposed to do.

Sucking in another breath, she started the car. She eased her foot from the brake, and then the clutch while gently pushing the gas. The car lurched forward and ground to a halt.

The sound Hank made from the passenger's seat was a mix between a choke and chuckle.

Murphy squeezed her eyes shut. Two seconds in and she'd already broken the car. Looked like even if there were kids playing at the park she wouldn't have to worry about any accidents. She couldn't even get the card to go forward.

"It's okay. It's okay." His reassurance was comforting but did nothing to stop her pounding heart.

Murphy wasn't sure if he was trying to convince her or himself. "This is such a bad idea."

"No, it's not. You'll get it," he encouraged. "Try again."

Not sure she really wanted to, Murphy started the car. With shaky legs, she managed to ease on the gas feeling a little brave at Hank's confidence in her.

This time the car moved a few feet before dying.

After another hour and countless times of stalling the

car, Murphy was able to drive around the parking lot, changing gears, without killing the engine.

Her legs started to feel solid again, and she was sure her heart wasn't about to thump out of her chest. She was doing it! She was actually driving!

"Cain, I do believe you're ready drive us home," Hank declared leaning back in his chair, hands propped behind his head.

Murphy's heart plummeted back to the floorboard. "You aren't serious." The idea of driving ten minutes back to the Harrington house, with the possibility of traffic, even just one other car, was both exciting and terrifying. There was also one other little problem. "I don't have my license, Hank. I probably shouldn't actually drive on real roads."

Hank shrugged. "Meh. It's not that far. We're not going to get pulled over. If you see flashing lights, just floor it."

"What?" Murphy squeaked. Forgetting what she was supposed to do next, both feet slammed on the break bringing the car to a dead stop.

Hank grinned. "Just kidding, Cain. You're not going to get pulled over. Go the speed limit. Make sure you have your seat belt on. Drive in a straight line. You'll be fine."

"You are so not funny," Murphy deadpanned ignoring the way her heart soared at his belief in her. Against her better judgement, she started the car back up and pulled out on Major Bass Drive, pointing the car toward the Harrington House. It wasn't like if she got caught driving without a license she would get in trouble with the police and be kicked out of Iverson. Actually, that's *exactly* what it would be like. Try as she might, Murphy couldn't stop thinking about getting kicked out of Iverson. Where would she go? What would happen to her then? By the time she turned off Major Bass, Murphy's legs had turned back to mush and she was sucking in way too many breaths, way too fast.

Nickleback Creek Hill was the only thing between her and getting out of the car. She was vaguely aware of Hank giving her some kind of instruction, but he sounded more like the teacher from the Charlie Brown Christmas special. Wa-wa-wa. She was halfway up the hill before she realized the car was slowing down despite the gas pedal being almost to the floor.

The harder Murphy pushed the gas, the slower they seemed to be going. Creeping up the hill. The car kept sputtering as if it was about to die. She couldn't let the car die. If it died, they'd roll backwards. "Hank! What's going on with this car?"

"You're going to have to down shift, Cain. Just push in the clutch and move to second gear."

Murphy wasn't sure if she should be relieved or infuriated by Hank's calmness. This was definitely the time to panic. She hated driving. This was such a horrible, awful, no good — Murphy downshifted, trying not to completely panic when the car rolled backwards a few inches before she pushed the gas in. The car jumped forward like the twins after downing a Red Bull.

"Great job, Cain." Hank praised, patting her on the shoulder. "Hills are the hardest part."

Murphy was still too worked up to notice the tingles shooting down her arm from where Hank touched her. "I hate driving." She remarked, probably much to Hank's chagrin.

———

"I'M NEVER, ever, *ever* driving again."

Ten minutes later, Murphy finally got the car up the hill (three times because Hank made her go back and drive it again, and again, to make sure she knew what she was doing) and parked at the Harrington House. She couldn't get out fast enough due to her jelly legs.

"Come on, Cain. You're slightly pale," Hank playfully pushed at her shoulder. "It wasn't that bad."

Murphy shot him a look as she tried to pinch color back into her cheeks. As proud as she was that she finally could say she'd driven a car, she was in no hurry to try it again. The twins would never believe her and that was fine by her.

"Ah, Master Hank," Jarvis greeted them as they burst through the front door.

Murphy shrugged out of her coat and handed it to his waiting arms. Biting her lip, she offered the butler a weak smile. She promised herself she wouldn't come back here, and yet here she was once again.

Hank rambled on, voice echoing off the high ceilings, about why she shouldn't be giving up on the whole driving thing.

"Tell her I'm right, Jarvis!" Hank said, desperately trying to find someone to back him up.

"I wouldn't know, sir," her responded taking Hank's coat and draping it on a hanger. Murphy warmed, Jarvis obviously taking her side.

Hank pulled at his hair. "Can I get no love?"

"However, sir," Jarvis went on, ignoring Hank's tantrum. "Madam Harrington's father has arrived and is currently waiting in Master Tripp's downstairs room."

"Grandpa Jack!" Hank clapped his hands together and started down the hall. "Awesome. Come on, Cain. If you won't listen to reason, I know you'll listen to Grandpa Jack."

Murphy knew for sure she wasn't at all ready to meet

any more of the Harrington family. That would be taking it too far. Meeting extended family felt a little too intimate. She tucked a stray hair behind her ear and straightened her rumpled Iverson sweatshirt. Seeing her hesitation, Jarvis held Murphy's coat out to her, with raised eyebrows.

"I should just go," Murphy tugged the coat on, pulling her hair from her collar.

"Wait. What?" Hank stopped midway down the hall and turned back. "You're leaving? Why? Mother has been prepping for Tripp's arrival all morning. Now Grandpa Jack's here."

"Right. Your grandfather is here." Murphy motioned up the hall. "You should go visit him. You don't need me hanging around."

Even though she really would have liked to see Tripp. She'd visit tomorrow. It meant another trip to the Harrington House. She already made the decision not to stay away. Already had a fight with Emmaline over the issue. This is what she wanted. "It's fine. I'll be back tomorrow." She shrugged. "Or something."

Twisting the bronze nob at the front door, Murphy was already preparing herself for the cold walk over the hill to Iverson. Two miles really wasn't that bad, she told herself. It was balmy outside, at least a good four degrees warmer than it had been most days that week.

"Cain, if you don't stop being ridiculous, I will throw you over my shoulder and carry you in to meet Grandpa Jack." Hank's teasing stopped her.

Her eyes slid closed. She leaned her forehead on the door. If he only knew who she really was, he wouldn't think she was being ridiculous. But wasn't this what she really wanted? She did say she wanted to be one of the in crowd— hot boyfriend and all. Even if it would only be for a little while. She would prove to everyone that she could be this person. She turned back around, letting the door close.

"I guess I can stay for a few minutes." She said taking her coat back off, and handing it over once again. "Besides, I *did* want to see Tripp."

"Perfect. Jarvis, could you have some coffee sent up for Murphy? Extra hot and extra delicious. She deserves it." Hank started back down the hall, talking over his shoulder as he went. "Oh, Jarvis, did everything go okay with Tripp's arrival? No complications?"

The butler appeared from around the corner. "Yes, sir. He and his nurses arrived within the last hour. And, sir," he paused as if not sure he should go on. "Madam Harrington does not yet know of Mr. Jones' arrival."

Hank winced. "Oh. This is going to be a good one. Come on, Cain, if you're here the fall out won't be quite as bad."

Murphy had to double-time to catch up with Hank's long strides down the hall. "Fall out? What do you mean?" She suddenly had the feeling she should be wearing battle armor to meet Grandpa Jack.

Pausing at the door to Tripp's room, Hank turned back, eyebrows raised. "You'll see." He winked and disappeared through the door.

CHAPTER NINE

THE FIRST THING Murphy noticed about Grandpa Jack was his size. Not that he was a particularly large man, he wasn't. In fact, he wasn't that much taller than Murphy. The hair on top of his head stood straight up and was snowy white giving Einstein a run for his money. His blue eyes had the same mischievous sparkle as Hank's. And if Murphy thought Hank was loud before, Grandpa Jack only increased the volume.

"Oh! My boy! My boy!" Grandpa Jack had jumped up from the wingback chair he was sitting in next to Tripp's bed and pulled Hank into a hug. Hank dwarfed his Grandfather who took a step back, holding Hank at arm's length. "It's been too long since I've seen your face. Let me take a look at you." He put one hand on either side of Hank's face and moved it back and forth in the light as if trying to find a blemish. "See what that Scottish air's been doing to ye." He chuckled at his fake (terrible) Scottish accent.

"Murphy!" Eloise, who had been sitting in a wingback chair next to Grandpa Jack's, jumped up when she spotted Murphy behind Hank. Stepping around a card table between their chairs, she threw her arms around Murphy. A little taken aback at Eloise's affection, Murphy returned the hug.

Murphy had hoped to stay in the background. She imagined visiting Tripp while Hank chatted with his Grandfather. They would be lost in conversation and Murphy would slip out and head home.

So much for that plan.

"Grandpa Jack, you have to meet Murphy." Eloise tugged on Murphy's arm practically dragging her from her hiding place behind Hank.

"Who do we have here?" Grandpa Jack clasped his hands together behind his back. "Murphy was it? You are simply beautiful."

"Good ol' Tripp had been keeping her a secret from us. Found out in the hospital it was actually her quick thinking that saved his life."

Eloise sighed and tucked her hands under her chin. "It's so romantic."

Murphy ducked her head not used to flattery. "Really, it was nothing. I was just doing what anyone would do."

"Whether or not they would have, I'm grateful that you were able to think quickly and save our Tripp's life," Grandpa Jack pulled her into an embrace. He smelled of peppermint and tobacco.

"Daddy?" Tabitha Harrington's splutter broke apart their hug, but not before Grandpa Jack mumbled something about sending out the cannons and girding your loins. Murphy bit her lip to keep from smiling. She liked him already.

"Tabitha, my darling girl." Grandpa Jack, not waiting for an invitation, hugged his daughter — if one could call hugging a board a hug. Tabitha looked even more ridged than normal.

"Wh-what are you doing here?"

Grandpa Jack stuffed his hands into his sweater pockets. "Well, Tabitha, my grandson is in a coma, and I hadn't seen my family in over two years. Besides it's Christmas time. And Christmas time is family time."

Tabitha blinked. "Tripp is just fine, Daddy. I would have called if it was something serious."

Grandpa Jack, Hank, Murphy, and Eloise all stared at Tabitha. Fine? Nothing serious? Murphy would like to know what Tabitha Harrington considered serious.

"Be that as it may," Grandpa Jack said patting Tabitha on the shoulder and pulling a pipe out of his back pocket. "I'm here to visit my daughter and grandchildren for Christmas. I hope you don't mind. I'm staying down the hall in the … what do you call it?" He looked over for help from Eloise.

"The Maple room, Grandpa."

"Yes, the Maple room." He put the pipe to his lips and chewed on the end.

"Daddy, I absolutely refuse to let you smoke in the house, and definitely not in the same room as Tripp." Tabitha squared her shoulders pulling back some of her composure.

Grandpa Jack tapped his daughter on the shoulder with the bowl of his pipe. "Tabitha, I haven't lit this thing in thirty-five years. It's only here for show."

"Yes, well, see that it is." Tabitha turned on her heel and click-clacked out the door and back down the hall.

"How in the world did my daughter end up like that?" Grandpa Jack asked staring at the empty door she had just walked through. "But enough of that. Come on, Hank, Murphy, I'm currently smearing your brother and sister in the game of rummy." He turned back to their card game, pipe still firmly between his lips.

"You are not! I was so beating you that time," Eloise protested swiping her cards from the table before her grandfather could peek at them. "And Tripp hardly counts!"

"Tripp really is a terrible card player." He agreed, grabbing the cards that had been placed in Tripp's hand and stacking them on the main deck. He proceeded to shuffle before holding his hand out for Eloise's cards as well. She rolled her eyes and smacked them on top of the deck.

Murphy sat on the end of Tripp's bed, careful not bounce too much. Not like it would matter. It was a very stiff California King and Tripp laid in the middle of it. It made him look more like a little boy than the teenager he was. A lock of hair had fallen over his forehead and Murphy fought the urge to lean over and brush it back. For once, Murphy hoped Tripp wouldn't wake up. The realization startled her. She really had been enjoying hanging out with Hank and Eloise and knew that Grandpa Jack was going to be just as fun. Besides, Murphy had a feeling this was going to be an epic card game and she really didn't want to miss it.

Hank sat beside her while Grandpa Jack moved the card table to the center of their awkwardly seated circle.

Dealing out the cards, Grandpa Jack, after double checking to make sure the door behind them was still closed, nodded to Eloise. She reached down and pulled out a pipe from the side of the chair, while Grandpa Jack produced three extras. He handed one to each of the card players and reached over and propped one in Tripp's mouth. "Gotta have the right tools to play cards," he said in way of explanation.

Following suit, Murphy put the pipe between her lips.

This had to be the strangest game of cards she had ever played—and she loved it.

"You gotta be careful with this one," Eloise whispered from behind her fan of cards, pointing at Grandpa Jack with her pipe while he went through the rules of the game. "He cheats."

"Dang right I do." Grandpa Jack proudly proclaimed, thumping the table. "Watch and learn, children, watch and learn."

———

MURPHY COMPLETELY LOST track of time—which seemed to be a theme when she hung out with the Harringtons. After losing three games of rummy (two to Grandpa Jack and one to Eloise—Hank was as bad at cards as she was) she realized it had already started getting dark. She prepared for the cold walk across the grounds back to Iverson, when Grandpa Jack all but demanded Hank give her a ride home.

"Don't worry, Grandpa Jack," Hank said helping Murphy into her coat. "I wasn't planning on letting her walk."

"Glad to see there are still gentlemen in the world." Grandpa Jack mumbled. Arm around Eloise, the two headed back down the hall. Murphy could hear their plans of a Christmas movie (was Die Hard considered a Christmas movie?) and popcorn.

Hank pulled on a hoodie and wrapped a scarf around his neck before opening the door. He tossed Murphy the keys. "Wanna drive home, Cain?"

Murphy tossed the keys right back at him. "That's real funny, Harrington."

"Harrington?" Hank stood up a little straighter. "I feel like I'm getting into trouble."

"I have a feeling you stay in trouble," Murphy laughed.

They were silent on the way back to Iverson. Murphy thought it strange how comfortable she and Hank were in each other's presence. They had just met last week, and under less than ideal circumstances. Still, Murphy was glad she had found a friend. She'd probably need a new one since Emmaline had decided to stop talking to her. Murphy's heart sunk when she remembered why they weren't talking. When everything was said and done, Hank shouldn't be talking to her either. She bit her lip until it stung. She looked at Hank's profile, face glowing green from the dashboard lights. She should tell him who she really was.

No, she wasn't going to do it. No one believed she could fit in. What—because she scrubbed toilets, she couldn't be someone that hung out with them? That was a load of crap, and she'd prove everyone wrong. She liked the Harringtons and it seemed they liked her back.

"Why the long face, Cain?" Hank reached over and squeezed her hand. "You did good today."

Murphy had the smallest pinch in the back of her brain to tell him, exactly what was on her mind, but she pushed the thought aside and instead replied, "Just tired, I guess. My best friend and I got into an argument last night."

"Want to talk about it?" Out of the corner of her eye, Murphy could see Hank's head moving between looking at her and the road.

Did she want to talk about it? She'd rather watch polish on Claire's nails dry. "Not really."

"Ok, then, how about you tell me why you don't want to ever drive again. It wasn't that bad, and besides, you graduate in what? A couple of months? What are you going to do then?"

She wasn't going to correct him about when she was graduating. Thanks to being held back, she still had a year left. No matter how hard she worked. "There is such thing as Uber, genius. And I want to move around. Not stay anywhere for too long. A car would just be an inconvenience." Her teeth chattered and she wasn't sure if it was from being cold or her nerves that were constantly on edge.

"Running from the law huh?" Hank joked. He turned the heat on high, warming more than just Murphy's chill.

"Nope. I just want to see the world. I want to see it all." Murphy wasn't sure how much she could share without sharing too much, but her head and heart had two different ideas. "When I was little, my dad and I had this map on the wall. It was huge. During the week, I would go to the library after school while he was working and get stacks of books on different locations around the world. On the weekend, after a breakfast of all-we-could eat pancakes, Dad's specialty, I would give him a report on the places I'd researched and we would add push pins to the places we wanted to travel to."

"That sounds amazing. But, hey, Tripp's favorite thing is globe hopping. And, last time I checked, he can drive, so maybe you wouldn't have to Uber around all that much."

"True." Murphy swallowed. Right. Tripp. Her boyfriend.

"So how old were you when you started going to Iverson?" Hank asked breaking into her thoughts.

It had been so long ago and yet it still felt like yesterday. "Eleven."

Murphy had been one of the "in" crowd then, but all that changed when she moved downstairs.

Hank pulled into the Iverson drive, the streetlamps

marking the way to the school. Pulling through the round drive, he put the car in park at the bottom of the steps and turned to face her.

"I had fun today."

"Me too, but," she pointed a finger at Hank. "I'm still pretty sure I'm never going to drive again."

Hank nudged her shoulder. "Ah, come on, Cain. Maybe it'll grow on you. With practice." Murphy chuckled, shaking her head. "I have no desire to get back behind the wheel of a car. Thank you very much."

Rolling his eyes, Hank replied. "Whatever you say, Cain."

"But really. Thank you for today. It's been a long time since I've had that much fun and thank you for introducing me to Grandpa Jack."

"He's a hoot. Gotta love him."

"He was something else." Murphy stuck her hands into her coat pockets, not really ready to leave the finally-warm car to dash inside. With a sigh, she relented. There was still the matter of checking in with Mrs. Potts. "Well, I'll see ya."

"Murphy," Hank grabbed her coat sleeve before she had time to push out of the car. She sank back into the seat.

"Yeah?"

"You busy tomorrow?"

Tomorrow was Thursday. The day she was planning on going on the weekly shopping trip with Mrs. Potts. But if Hank had plans, she was sure she could fit everything in. "Not much. What's up?"

"Wheezy and I have some Christmas shopping to do. She wanted to know if you would tag along. We'd be going tomorrow afternoon, say 2ish?"

"Cutting it a little close, aren't you?"

"Yeah, yeah, I do every year. I'm whatcha call, fashionably late." Hank ran a hand through his hair.

Murphy chewed on her bottom lip. She was throwing the promise to herself out the window. Forget that. She was lighting that promise on fire and dancing around the flames. No, she definitely shouldn't go shopping. All the other times had just been accidents forced by Hank. But this would be all her. The answer had to be no. Didn't it?

"Yeah, I think I could do that."

Hank's face lit up. "Great. We'll swing by and pick you up. Now go on and get inside. It's cold out here. I won't leave until I see you've made it inside."

Whoever said chivalry was dead? Murphy tucked her head down against the cold and jogged up the stairs pulling the heavy oak door open. She turned and waved to Hank has he pulled back down the drive.

Once inside she leaned up against the door. Heaven help her she was getting in over her head.

NOTIFICATION CENTER

Message from Eloise Harrington (10:53 PM)

Hank told me your going with us tomorrow! I am soooooooooooo excited!!!!

Message from Eloise Harrington (10:57 PM)

I totally forgot to ask how driving went! Hank said you did great. Yay! Go you.

CHAPTER TEN

MRS. POTTS HAD PRACTICALLY SQUEALED when Murphy asked her about the Christmas shopping trip with Hank and Eloise. Murphy figured the excitement had something to do with the fact that, for the first time, Murphy actually had an interest outside of school, work, and the occasional video game crafted by the Taylor brothers.

The older woman even tried to shove a couple of bills into Murphy's hand, telling her that she needed to have fun and shouldn't have to worry about something as silly as money. After a back and forth argument, Murphy accepted the gift, but when Mrs Potts' back was turned, slipped it back into the jar where she kept her emergency funds.

Since the weekly trip to the grocery store with Mrs. Potts was one of Murphy's favorite tasks and she was generally in classes during the day, it was one chore she actually looked forward to during breaks. Thankfully, Mrs. Potts was eager to leave a little earlier than normal, especially since she wanted to be home to get her afternoon coffee and snack made before her soap opera came on.

As they drove toward the store Mrs. Potts asked, "He actually taught you how to drive a standard?"

Murphy regaled the woman with the entire ordeal—including getting stuck on the hill and her declaration of never wanting to get behind the wheel again, which had Mrs. Potts shaking with laughter.

"Oh, Murphy," said Mrs. Potts when she could finally catch her breath. "I do hope one day you'll be able to try again under less dramatic situations."

Murphy shook her head. "Not likely."

"Amos or I should have taken the time to teach you." Her tone hinted at regret. "You should have told us that you had an interest in learning to drive. We would have somehow made it happen. Surely Sonora couldn't have found fault with you learning that life skill."

"It's ok, Mrs. P. Really," Murphy shrugged. "I didn't have a desire to learn how to drive. It just kind of happened. It was like Hank made it his life mission or something."

"That boy is good for you," Mrs. Potts smiled turning into the box store parking lot. Save for three other cars, the parking lot was empty.

Murphy could feel her face heat, as she buried deeper into her scarf and coat, wishing she would have remembered to grab her hat. No, it was Tripp that was good for her. Not Hank.

Right?

She shook her head as though that would knock Hank from her thoughts.

The duo tromped across the parking lot basking in the warmth of the sun.

"Oh, the twins missed you at breakfast." Mrs. Potts mentioned. "Something about wanting you to swing by and check out Sir Siegfried 2.0?"

Murphy laughed. "It's the new game they are attempting to create. The first level was supposed to be a challenge, but I accidentally breezed right through it," she explained. "Anyway, this morning I just couldn't wake up. I'm sorry I missed helping with breakfast prep."

Mrs. Potts waved her arm. "Pish posh, dear. You've had a lot going on. You've had many early mornings. I'm glad you got some sleep."

She appreciated Mrs. P's slack on the rules, but that wasn't an excuse to be slacking on her job. Leaving her responsibilities for Mrs. Potts. It wasn't right — never mind that if Headmistress Kingfisher found out Murphy would be in so much trouble.

"Besides," Mrs. Potts continued. "There's only a few students to prep for. Hardly a challenge."

Frowning, she picked at a thread that had unraveled on her coat. It better not be falling apart — not that she wasn't expecting it. The coat was older than she was.

Since they had a weekly shopping date, or rather, Mrs. Potts had a weekly shopping date, most of the items were already pulled for the school, it simply had to be picked up.

Before the final check out, Mrs. Potts pulled Murphy over to the bakery and made her choose a donut from the case. Frosted blueberry cake donut. Blueberry anything was always Murphy's favorite. If she closed her eyes and thought hard enough, she could almost taste the blueberry pancakes her dad once made. Always an extra two blueberries for the eyes and six for the mouth and of course a spray of whipped cream for hair.

Mumbling her thanks to the baker, Murphy took the paper wrapped donut and Styrofoam cup of steaming coffee. Mmmm coffee. Of course, she hadn't gotten up early enough to drink a cup, even if Mrs. Potts had it sitting on the counter ready to go. That's what she got for slacking.

She had to figure out a way to juggle everything better.

Mrs. Potts put the groceries on the school account and a bag boy followed them out to the van and loaded it up. They sat in the car, the heater on full blast, quiet while they both nibbled on their donuts and sipped coffee that was too hot.

"Don't forget about finishing the cleaning on the sixth floor. Should be a good week to get it done." Mrs. Potts mused.

The sixth floor. Emmaline and Claire's floor. The sixth floor always needed the extra cleaning while the students were away. With the exception of Emmaline and a couple of boys from Spain, most of the students on that floor were slobs. She had already unintentionally started on Tripp's room thanks to Fiona. Speaking of that pesky cat, she was running low on food and litter. She'd have to remember to grab some while she was out this afternoon.

As soon as the Iverson van pulled around to the kitchen entrance, Floyd and Lloyd bounded out the door. They stood like two footmen from Downton waiting to assist the girls' every need.

"What are you two boys up to now, Mmm?" Mrs. Potts regarded them with raised eyebrows waiting for the prank to drop.

The twins exchanged a glance making Murphy wonder. They *were* up to something.

"The Royal Ms. Murphy Cain has a visitor in the front hall," Floyd cleared his throat and announced.

It was Murphy and Mrs. Potts turn to exchange a confused glance.

"You boys stop funning and tell us what's going on," Mrs. Potts scolded.

Lloyd rolled his eyes. "Pretty boy Harrington is here to see Murph."

"What?" Murphy looked at her watch. He was an hour and a half early. She looked down at her grimy jeans and dirty shoes inwardly groaning. This double life was going to kill her.

Mrs. Potts flew into action. "Boys, how long has he been waiting?"

"Five minutes tops."

"Right. Murphy dear, you go change and use the back stairs so you can enter from the main staircase. Boys," she tossed Lloyd the keys to the van — which Murphy wondered how smart that decision was. "I need you to unload the van. No driving."

Floyd snickered until Mrs. Potts threatened to give them only bread and water for the remaining time of the break. She was just kidding. At least Murphy *thought* she was. "And I'll go and see if Mr. Harrington needs anything. Ready? Let's go."

Everyone jumped into action. The twins, for whatever reason, ran in circles before running to the back of the van. Mrs. Potts spoofed her short grey hair and smoothed her sweater and skirt before squaring her shoulders and marching inside like a solider heading into battle.

Murphy stood, frozen in place, blinking back tears. She was going to be leaving Mrs. Potts again with most of the housework. But oh, how she wanted to go. She wanted to not worry about cleaning and doing someone else's laundry and the dozen other tasks Headmistress Kingfisher had assigned to her. She wanted to hang out with Hank and Wheezy on the town, Christmas shopping like a regular seventeen-year-old. She wanted to pretend that she belonged. Mrs. Potts, it seemed, wanted her to as much as she did, so why did Murphy feel so guilty?

"Murph, get a move on! Can't keep him waiting!" One twin shouted from behind an industrial sized box of toilet paper.

Silly grin on her face, she scrambled inside stumbling into her room. Fire and ice pulsing in her veins.

She kicked her shoes across the room and shimmied out of her jeans. She prayed her nicer pair were clean. Digging through her basket of clothes, she pulled out her favorite hunter-green long-sleeved tee-shirt and (yes!) her clean jeans. She pulled on a pair of socks (her lucky mismatched Doctor Who pair) and her grimy Cons — there was nothing she could do about that. Looking at herself in the mirror hanging on the back of the door, she grabbed a tube of lip gloss and dabbed it over her lips with her pinkie. She ran her fingers through her hair and tucked it behind her ears. She rolled her eyes at herself. Seriously what was she doing?

She wiped the lip gloss off and rubbed it on her jeans. She pulled her hair up into a messy pony and dared one last inspection in the mirror. Better.

Tucking her coat over her arm, Murphy glanced one more time at the disaster she left behind. Her room was starting to look like *it* belonged on the sixth floor. She really needed to take time to clean it up before it started giving her a tick. The past week she had been so busy between keeping her double lives straight, that she hadn't even had time to put away her clean clothes — one of her pet peeves. Sighing she gave Fiona's ears a scratch and let the door close behind her. That was a mess for another day.

She took the service stairs two at a time, pausing at the

top to catch her breath and smooth down pieces of stubborn hair that wouldn't stay in place.

She could hear Mrs. Potts prattling on about something and Hank's polite agreement. And then she heard other voices. Waffles and cheese! Floyd and Lloyd were chatting him up as well.

"Murphy, did you know this guy has a room full of vintage arcade games?" Lloyd asked when she came into view at the stairs.

"I did," Murphy skipped down the last two steps. "And I've played on them. You're super early." She turned to Hank, praying that her "relationship" with Tripp hadn't been discussed.

Hank shrugged his shoulders. "Wheezy was chomping at the bit to get going. Ready?"

"Sure," Murphy said shifting her bag on her shoulder.

There was an audible groan from both the twins and a hush from Mrs. Potts when Murphy and Hank turned to leave.

"Goodbye, Mrs. P. Boys," Murphy said practically pulling Hank toward the door.

"Murph, you have to bring him over so we can show him our games! And—" Floyd yelled out, the rest of whatever he was going to say cut off by the door.

Shaking her head, Murphy put on her jacket, stamping her feet against the cold.

Hank chuckled. "Love your friends."

"Floyd and Lloyd? Yeah, they are awesome." She did love them, and she was fairly certain they would hit it off with Hank. She just wasn't sure they wouldn't accidently tell her secret. The one *she* needed to tell.

In the back of Hank's Range Rover, Eloise was having her own dance party. Murphy could hear the beat of her pop music blaring through the closed windows. She stopped and waved when she caught them watching.

"Hey, Wheezy," Murphy greeted sliding into the front seat while Hank jogged around to the driver's side after double checking that Murphy was sure she didn't want to drive.

"Okay, girls. Let's get this shopping thing done." Hank turned out of Iverson's drive in the direction of town.

It was busy for a Thursday afternoon, but then again Murphy should have expected that since it was the last weekend to shop before Christmas.

Wheezy picked up a couple things for her mom, and a tie for her dad — that she already declared that he'd never wear. Murphy picked up something small for Mrs. P and Mr. G's favorite lemon candy. She also picked up cat food and kitty litter that Hank had insisted on paying for. They had only been shopping for an hour before Hank decided that he was starving and it was time to eat.

They made their way to Bob and Ellie's. Murphy sent up a silent prayer that no one recognized her from visiting with Mr. G.

Twinkle lights flickered overhead, as a band played Christmas songs in the square. How they were able to keep their fingers moving in the cold, Murphy wasn't sure.

Eloise led them to a booth in front of the large windows so they could watch the festivities in the square. A waitress with a Santa hat came over and took their orders. Hamburgers for Hank and Wheezy, a plate of fries and a strawberry milkshake for Murphy. After scarfing down her meal, Wheezy slid out of the booth.

"I'll be right back."

Hank's eyebrows raised. "Okay?"

"I'll be right back, Hank," she repeated, she turned to

Murphy. "Keep him company, yeah? And whatever you guys do don't follow me." She started backing toward the door.

"Wheezy, wha—"

Eloise pointed her finger in his direction. "Hank. I'm getting your Christmas present." Her eyes darted toward the window. "And don't watch where I go either to try and figure it out." She turned on her heel and pushed out the door.

Hank looked out the window, following his sister with his gaze. Murphy picked up her napkin and tossed it at him. "Hey, play nice. Let your sister have this."

Shrugging, Hank took a long sip of his milkshake. "Just making sure she got across the street safely."

Murphy pursed her lips at him. The protectiveness of Hank for his sister set her heart fluttering. "Really? Hank, this is the square. What is she going to get run over by? A crazed shopper?"

"Hey, you never know." He picked up a fry and popped it in his mouth. Studying her, he asked, "So, Cain, what's your favorite subject in school?"

"Literature. Followed closely by creative writing. You?"

"History. Favorite color?"

Rapid fire questions. She narrowed her eyes. That's how they were going to play. "Red."

"You have an entire Saturday to watch your favorite show. What are you bingeing?"

"Doctor Who."

Hank's eyebrows shot up. "Really? Doctor Who?"

She nodded. "Yep. Now it's my turn. That was two for you and you still haven't answered."

"Blue and old school MacGyver."

"No way. MacGyver?"

"Total way."

"That is so lame." Murphy sank a fry into ranch before swiping it through the ketchup.

"What's lame is your eating habits. Ranch and ketchup? Who does that?"

Murphy smiled. "Don't knock it until you try it, Harrington."

Shaking his head, Hank leaned over on his elbows. "So. What deep dark secrets does Murphy Cain keep."

Bad time to take a gulp of her shake. Murphy choked. "Secrets?" she coughed out, eyes watering.

Hank passed her a napkin, chuckling. "I was just joking, Cain, but now you have me wondering."

"Sorry, I swallowed wrong," Murphy cleared her throat. *Now. Tell him now.* Her head was practically screaming. It was an open invitation to tell him about the *real* Murphy. And still, she really didn't want this to end. "What about you, Hank Harrington. What's your biggest secret?"

"Now who's not answering questions?" Hank sobered and stared out the window at the shoppers passing by laden down by bags with last minute gifts they'd spent way too much on. Murphy noticed Hank's tapered fingers fiddled with the straw sitting in vanilla milkshake turned melted mush. "I don't want to go into the family business," he confessed.

"What would you do instead?" Murphy used a fry to write her name in the drying blob of ketchup.

Sighing, Hank leaned back in the booth, arms draped over the sides. "If I could do anything, I'd just play the piano."

Goosebumps popped up on Murphy's arm. Music from her memories danced melodies through her mind. "You play piano?"

"Everyday since I was three." Hank picked up a fry and dragged it through a pile of ranch and ketchup before popping it in his mouth. He faked gagged. "That's disgusting, Cain."

She chuckled. "Overreact-er. So, you want to play professionally." She found herself lining up the fries left on her plate.

Hank nodded, around a mouthful of burger.

"Why can't you?"

Swallowing, Hank barked out a bitter laugh. "My father would never go for that. He's convinced if he leaves the company to Tripp, he'll just run it into the ground."

"Seriously?" Now that she thought about it, she couldn't really see Tripp as the CEO of a fortune 500 company, but wasn't that the sort of thing someone could grow into? Learn to do?

"Sorry, I hope you weren't counting on Tripp being the sole heir or anything like that." Hank rolled his eyes. "Apparently, I'm Richard Harrington's last hope."

Choosing to ignore the Tripp-jab she went on. "Why don't you just tell your dad you don't want the company. Wouldn't he want you to follow your heart?"

"Oh sure," Hank pushed his plate toward the end of the table and leaned on his elbows. "Hey, Dad I'm just going to forget all the plans you've had for me and become a pianist. Murph, that'd go over like lead."

"What about Eloise," Murphy motioned to the direction Eloise had disappeared. "It's the twenty-first century, female CEOs aren't unheard of. She would totally rock it and *she* could be the last hope of Richard Harrington."

"Wheezy would love that, but Dad doesn't see it that way." Hank rolled his eyes, shrugging. "Being a pianist is just one of those pipe dreams, never going to happen."

"I still think you should talk to him," Murphy pushed. "He's your father. He wants you to be happy, right?"

Hank let out a long sigh, hand raking down his face. "Let's just drop it. Me and the piano just aren't meant to be."

Murphy swallowed not liking the fact that it sounded like Hank was already giving up on his dream without a fight. She took a long draw from her milkshake giving herself a brain freeze.

"Waffles, that hurts." She clutched her head. What was she supposed to do when getting brain freeze? Drink more cold stuff? Breathe out like a dragon? Push the tongue to the roof of her mouth?

"Brain freeze?" Chuckling, Hank leaned over the table, holding out Eloise's cup of melted ice water.

Murphy shot him a confused look.

"Just trust me."

Murphy slurped down few gulps of water, surprised when her headache began to subside.

"Better?" Hank sat back a smug look on his face.

Murphy dipped her fingers in the water and flicked it toward Hank.

"Hey now!" Hank pretended to shake water off himself. "That's just rotten. You try to help a girl out, and this is the thanks you get."

"At least it wasn't food."

"True that." Hank slid out of the booth. "Come on. Let's go find Wheezy. Mom's going to expect us home soon."

They grabbed their coats from the stand by the door. Hank shrugged into his before helping Murphy with hers.

They pushed out into the cold afternoon. Murphy was pretty sure it was colder than when they sat down for lunch.

She groaned inwardly knowing that, with the dropping temps, snow couldn't be far behind. At least it would be pretty.

They didn't get far down the sidewalk before they spotted Wheezy trudging toward them, arms loaded down with bags. She had done some serious shopping in the last twenty-five minutes.

"Wheezy, what in the world?" Hank met her tugging the bags from her arms. "I thought you said you only had a couple stops left! You must have bought out the stores!"

Eloise shook her arms at her sides. Relief washed on her face not having the load of bags any longer. "I did, but then I thought of a few more things I needed. Stop trying to peek in the bags! Your gift is in there." Eloise swatted her brother as he tried to bend to see what was in the bags he was carrying.

"You should have told us. We could have come helped you." Murphy felt bad she and Hank had been sitting and visiting in the warm cafe while Eloise had been drowning under bags and boxes.

Eloise waved her off. "It's really not so bad."

"But still—" Murphy was cut off by the shrill tone of Hank's cell phone.

Glancing at the caller ID, Hank grimaced.

"Girls, our time has come to an end. Mommy dearest calls."

CHAPTER ELEVEN

MURPHY NEEDED to make things right with Emmaline. She was barely sleeping and refused to believe it was because of their fight. News flash. It totally was. Murphy knew that she should just shrug it off as part of her old life, maybe going forward Emmaline wouldn't be there, but that just felt so final. Maybe if she talked it over with someone who was in the thick of things with her—whether he knew it or not—she would feel better.

Slipping on an old Bon Jovi t-shirt, another item of clothing saved from her dad's closet, over a long-sleeved shirt, she tugged on her coat. Tying a scarf around her neck, she pulled a wool beanie down over her ears. At the last minute, Murphy tucked Fiona into her coat. The visit would do Tripp good. She would just have to make sure Mrs. Harrington didn't find out. She tiptoed across the kitchen, trying to remember what Mrs. Potts' morning routine was. If she was caught, she'd just say she was going for an early run. With a cat. Because that seemed logical.

Murphy squared her shoulders to bear the cold before pulling open the door. Glad she had remembered to put on the wool socks that Mr. Gruber had given her, she kicked at the dead leaves and pine needles on the lawn. The sun was just coming up painting the sky with brilliant oranges and pinks.

It was much quicker to get to the Harrington house by cutting through the green, jumping over the sad excuse for a property fence, and swimming through the trees that bordered the entire Harrington property. Thirty-five minutes later she was stomping on the Harrington steps trying to get feeling back into her legs. At least Fiona seemed to enjoy the trip as she was snuggled up against Murphy, purring.

Murphy was only a little surprised that Jarvis swung the door open before she had a chance to knock, looking as if he had been expecting her.

"Good morning, Ms. Cain," Jarvis bowed at the waist and helped Murphy remove layers, startling, and quickly recovering at the sight of Fiona.

"Good morning, Jarvis." Murphy slipped off her Cons, damp from the morning dew. Balancing Fiona in her arms, and praying she didn't decide to bolt, Murphy placed them by the door, knowing that the capable butler would probably stash them in a closet until she was ready to return home. "I was just going to visit with Tripp if it's ok."

Jarvis bowed his head as if a girl coming over unannounced with a cat before breakfast was the most normal thing in the world.

"Yes, Miss. I'll bring some of Mrs. George's hot coffee. Unless you'd prefer cocoa or tea?"

"Coffee would be marvelous."

Murphy made her way down the hall toward Tripp's room. She pushed the door silently open, gasping to see Grandpa Jack sitting next to Tripp's bed reading a paperback by the light of a lamp. He glanced up, putting a bookmark in his book, and placed his glasses on top of his head.

"Good morning, Murphy dear. I was expecting the nurse. Is it morning already?" He put his book down on the side table and stretched glancing out the large bay window into the dark.

"Barely," Murphy smiled, putting Fiona on the bed. "I brought a friend for a visit."

Grandpa Jack stood up from his seat and offered it to Murphy. "I'll let you two young people, and feline, visit," he stroked down Fiona's back who arched to his hand. He chuckled. "I'm going to go in search of some coffee and breakfast. I hear Mrs. George has some of the best pastries around these parts."

He patted her arm before silently crossing the room and closing the door behind him. Now that Murphy was here, her mouth felt oddly dry. It wasn't as if Tripp was actually going to respond to what she had to say. It was basically like talking to a corpse. Not that Tripp was a corpse. Yet. Oh, waffles why would she think that?

She had practiced a speech the entire walk over. It had kept her mind off the fact that she was pretty sure her nose was freezing off her face. And here it was. Go time. Her stomach tightened, and she glanced over to the door making sure that it was closed before launching into what she had come to say.

"Hey, Tripp," Murphy whispered. Why was she whispering? It wasn't as if anyone would be up at this hour to eavesdrop on her confession — well, except apparently Jarvis and Grandpa Jack. But for some reason she felt like those two would keep her secret. Even if they did manage to overhear her barely-there whispering.

Fiona sniffed at the tubes flowing from her Master

before taking a paw and ever so gently pressing it to his face. When he didn't wake up, she curled up in the hollow of his neck and laid her head on his shoulder.

Murphy sucked in a deep breath, cleared her throat, and started again.

"Um," Murphy bit the inside of her cheek. She had never felt so awkward — and she had been in some weird situations, especially lately. She glanced over her shoulder at the still closed door. Maybe she hoped someone else would come in and save her from the confession. This room felt so big. The large windows covering three-fourths of the room probably had something to do with it. If she lived here, she'd want this to be her room. She loved that it overlooked the woods that surrounded the property. A squirrel bouncing over the leaves distracted her.

"So it's me. Murphy Cain. Again." Murphy chuckled. "Jarvis... I mean Jim... do you call him Jim or Jarvis. Is it only Hank who calls him Jarvis? Anyway, he let me in this morning. Good morning. I thought I'd come by and say hello before the day got started. And I think Fiona was missing you too. Don't tell your mom on me. Hank said she's not a fan." She was rambling. There was a tap at the door, and Jarvis walked in with a tray of coffee and what looked like at least four different type of muffins. "I thought you might want some breakfast as well, Ms. Cain."

"Thank you, Jarvis. This is a lot. I don't even know if I can eat all this before I need to head back to Iverson. I can't stay—"

Jarvis held up a hand, cutting off Murphy's objections. "That may be, but you can stay long enough to eat one of Cook's tasty muffins with your coffee while you warm up."

He placed the tray next on the side table. "The straw-berry cheesecake muffins are my personal favorite."

Murphy smiled her thanks as Jarvis bowed out of the room.

"Fiona is doing good." Murphy bit into the muffin as she gave Tripp the update. Her eyes slid closed and she moaned. This was good. "My room isn't as big as yours, but I don't think she minds. There aren't as many places that she can hide." Murphy chuckled to herself. She'd stowed the kitty litter in the bathroom and hid the food and water bowl in the little alcove between the dresser and wall under her bed. Fiona didn't seem to object. Her favorite place to perch was in Murphy's bed on her favorite fluffy blanket. "She was almost out of food so I had to pick some up when I went to town with your brother and sister yesterday. I couldn't find the brand that you've been feeding her, so I just got something that looked good. Hank wouldn't let me pay for it. You have a really good brother." *That is beside the point, Murphy. Get to what you were going to say and get out of here.*

Murphy wrapped her hands around the mug of coffee. She was colder than she thought. She took a sip trying to figure out what spices were added to it. Cinnamon? Nutmeg? Turmeric? She'd have to ask Mrs. George for the recipe. She drained the mug and set it back on the tray.

"Your whole family is nice. So welcoming. I know it's bad that I still haven't told anyone that I'm not really your girlfriend. It's just kind of nice to hang out with people who don't know where I come from. Who don't, you know, pity me." Murphy ran a hand through her hair, messing her pony. She freed it from the elastic tie and started braiding it over her shoulder.

"I know that doesn't make it right. Emmaline isn't even talking to me over it." Murphy pushed out a breath, refusing to cry. "I promise that before the break is over, I'll tell your family the truth. And I promise not to make this weird when you — everyone — gets back to school. In fact, if it's ok with you, we can just pretend that it never happened.

"Well, I hope you have a good day." Murphy felt silly has soon as she said it. "I mean ... have ... never mind."

Murphy picked up the tray and went to find Jarvis or Mrs. George, cradling Fiona in the nook of her arm. Balancing the tray on one hand, Murphy opened the door and tiptoed out into the hallway. Turning she almost ran into Hank, leaning against the wall. Who from the look of his mused hair, sleep pants, bare feet and newspaper under one arm looked as if he had just rolled out of bed and was on his way to visit Tripp.

"Good morning," he greeted her, pushing off the wall, a bemused look on his face.

"Oh! I'm so sorry." Murphy grabbed the tray with her other hand, dropping Fiona. Hank reached down and grabbed her before she darted away.

Her stomach dropped. Panic shot through her. How long had he been standing there? How much had he heard? But Hank's face melted into a smile instantly putting her to ease.

"You're here awfully early." Hank stated, amusement coloring his features as he petted Fiona, who as it seemed had finally warmed up to him.

Murphy shifted the tray and tucked a strand of hair behind her ear. Why couldn't it just stay in place? "I just thought Tripp might want a visit from Fiona, so we walked over this morning. Jarvis let me in."

Both teens nodded at a nurse, who looked at them, an eyebrow quizzically raised, as she passed into Tripp's room.

"You amaze me, Murphy Cain." Hank bopped his

newspaper on her head. "Are you heading out already?" He took the tray from her and handed Fiona back.

"Oh yes, I need to get back to help Mrs. Potts." The admission slipped out before Murphy could stop it. She hurried to move down the hall, praying Hank hadn't heard the admission.

Hank quirked an eyebrow. "You help the housekeeper?"

Murphy closed her eyes. She hated living in a lie. It seemed that she just kept getting deeper and deeper under. She pasted a smile on her face before turning to face him. "Yes, I do help the housekeeper every once in a while. Do you have a problem with that?"

Hank's grin made her belly do flip flops.

Stop that. She told herself. She hated her reaction to Hank.

Hank bit from one of the leftover muffins on the tray. "Not at all, Cain. Not at all."

Murphy gave him a curt nod and turned on her heel to escape.

———

MURPHY CHEWED ON HER THUMBNAIL, staring at her computer like it would self-combust at any moment. She paced back and forth in her tiny bedroom. If you could call it pacing. It was more like three steps in one direction, turn on a heel, three steps in the opposite direction.

She had to call Emmaline.

They had never gone more than a day without talking to each other. They were going on three days, and Murphy could barely stand it anymore. She still wasn't sleeping, felt sick to her stomach, and she was having trouble with her daily tasks. Although she wasn't sure if that was because of the distraction of not having talked with Emmaline, or the distraction over the hill that she kept visiting every free moment she had.

Looking at the clock and doing time conversion in her head for the hundredth time in the past minute, Murphy turned to Fiona who was perched on the bed cleaning herself.

"I should just do it, right?"

Fiona stared back at her mid-lick.

Murphy threw up her hands. "Great, now I'm talking to a cat! I'm just going to do it." Before she could second guest herself, Murphy punched the call button.

She went back to chewing on her nail.

It rang once, twice, three times.

"Come on, come on, pick up," Murphy muttered.

On the fifth ring, Emmaline's face appeared.

Murphy held up her hand in a sort of greeting. "Hey," she offered a tentative smile.

Emmaline studied her for a long second more before smiling back. "Hi."

"I'm sorry I—"

"Murphy, I'm sorry—"

Both girls spoke at the same time.

"You go first," Murphy said.

"No, you." Emmaline had moved closer to her computer so her face took up practically the entire screen.

Murphy took a deep breath. "Emmaline, I'm so sorry. I know you were only saying those things because you care that I don't get hurt. I've thought a lot about what you've said, and you are right but—"

"But you still haven't told the Harringtons the truth," Emmaline finished for her.

Murphy shook her head. "I will tell them. Eventually. I

promise. It's just the past week has been so amazing. They don't pity me. And I actually feel like I belong. I love hanging out with his family."

"Murph, you have me and the twins and Mrs. Potts and Mr. Gruber. What about us? We love you just the way you are. We've never made you feel less-than have we?"

"Never! But with them it's different," Murphy paused looking for the words to describe it. "I've been hanging out with Hank and Eloise and I really like him."

"Him?" Emmaline cocked an eyebrow, knowing grin on her face.

"Them! I like both of them." Murphy felt her face flush. Did she really just say she liked Hank? Out loud? It was totally just a slip.

"You seem happy," Emmaline hugged herself.

Murphy sighed. "Oh, I am."

"Okay, then I'm sorry too. I probably overstepped. It's really your decision what you do or don't tell them. I didn't want you to feel like you have to change who you are to fit in. I just don't want to see you hurt."

Murphy touched the screen. "I know you don't, Ems. I love you."

"I love you back," Emmaline shifted the screen, sitting in a more comfortable position. "Ok. Now. Dish about all the things you've been doing this week! I feel like we haven't talked in forever."

"It has been forever," Murphy jumped up onto her bed and pulled her laptop into her lap, pushing Fiona back to the pillow she had been sleeping on. "Ems, I learned to drive a car!" She squealed.

"Shut up!" Emmaline hugged a pillow to her, the always there can of Diet Coke in hand.

"Seriously! Hank decided that I needed to learn, so he

took me out to Pack's Landing parking lot and taught me in a couple hours. On a stick shift!"

"Oh my gosh, that's amazing. So, you're like a real driver and everything now."

"Absolutely not! I hated it. Hank's convinced I should try again, but there's no way."

"Hank again," Emmaline smiled. "What's going on there?"

"With Hank?" Murphy bit the inside of her cheek. "There's nothing going on with Hank. He thinks I'm Tripp's girlfriend."

"Mmhmm." Emmaline didn't sound convinced.

"Stop it. Seriously. There's nothing going on. Really. I promise I still crush on Tripp every chance I get." And if she didn't admit to her real feelings, maybe they would just go away. Hank was an infatuation since he'd been around so much lately.

"As long as you aren't having your movie scene fantasies about him."

"Of course not." And she hadn't. The realization shocked her a bit. "Tripp is still my leading man."

The girls burst into giggles. The giggles died away and Fiona had somehow made her way back to Murphy's lap. Murphy stroked her grey fur basking in the comfort of chatting with Emmaline.

"I've missed this," Murphy cut in on a story about some museum that Emmaline and her brother had gotten kicked out of because her brother had a sneezing fit over one of the statues and the guards had been convinced they were casing the place out and the sneezing fit was some kind of distraction.

"Me too, Murph. Let's not do it again, okay?" Emmaline touched her screen.

Murphy touched her screen back. "Agreed."

"I gotta go. Jamie is calling that he's hungry for dinner. I think we're going to get something from the food cart out on the street."

"Jamie's always hungry," Murphy laughed.

"True that."

Emmaline signed off. Murphy sighed. She wasn't sure what the rest of the week was going to bring but having her best friend back in her corner made it feel like at least something was right.

NOTIFICATION CENTER

Message from Hank Harrington (11:52 PM)

Hey! I forgot to mention it, but we're having a little Christmas thing on Christmas. Mom wanted to make sure you could come around 10:30… I'll pick you up. She didn't want you spending Christmas at Iverson by yourself.

Message from Murphy Cain (11:53 PM)

I don't know…

ELOISE HARRINGTON HAS ENTERED the chat

Message from Eloise Harrington (11:53 PM)

Pleeeeeeeeeeaaaaaaaaaaaasssssssssssseeeeeeeeeee?

Message from Murphy Cain (11:54 PM)

Ok. I'll come.

Message from Hank Harrington (11:54 PM)

Great! :)

Message from Eloise Harrington (11:54 PM)

Yessssss!!!!!!!!!!!!!!!!

CHAPTER TWELVE

MURPHY STRETCHED, basking in the mid-morning sun for the first time in a long time. Mercifully, she'd slept past nine, ignoring the birds chirping for her to wake with the sun.

Since making up with Emmaline, she felt light, like a weight had lifted from her shoulders. She was certain she never wanted to fight with her best friend again. It hurt her heart too much — not to mention her sleep.

Rolling out of bed, she stuffed her feet into oversized slippers and shuffled into the kitchen. Mrs. Potts and Mr. Gruber would be at church until at least noon. She pushed the button on the coffee maker and drummed her fingers on the counter as she waited for liquid gold to brew.

Somewhere in the front hall, Murphy heard the tinkling sounds of a piano. She frowned. Who would be playing the piano at this hour? She was sure the twins would be asleep for at least another two hours, and she didn't think anyone was left at Iverson who could play the piano. Not that the twins would play one even if they could.

Not waiting for the coffee maker to finish, Murphy

poured herself all of what had brewed and tiptoed out of the kitchen. Drawn to the sound, she let it catch her up in its web.

Swaying around the tables in the mess hall, she stepped into the grand hallway. Thankfully she'd remembered to put on her slippers. The chill bit at her skin. This part of the school wasn't newly insulated, but old and drafty, reminding her of an English manor. The melodic sounds of Clare d'Lune grew louder causing her chest to tighten. She stopped outside the front room where the piano was housed. The notes causing her eyes to close, lilting and sleepy.

Her father used to play her that song. For a fleeting moment, she held the ridiculous notion that she would see him when she rounded the corner. She knew it was silly. Pushing the thoughts away, she swallowed the emotion bubbling in the back of her throat and took a step around the corner.

Hank.

Her stomach did a flip flop. What was he doing here? And so early in the morning.

His broad back was straight and proud, his long fingers pressing gently together on the keys, making the too quiet beast stationed there sing. Just watching him she could tell he belonged at the piano.

Her feet took her across the room, the music a magnet, and she slid into the empty space beside him on the bench. Hank shifted over giving her room she didn't want. Murphy tucked her legs to her chest and wrapped chilled fingers around the warm cup of coffee. Steam danced upward to the music, tickling her cheeks and eyelashes.

The song ended and Murphy could feel her heart

beating steadily against her chest. Hank's quick breaths matching the rhythm.

"Please, don't stop," she whispered not wanting to talk, just wanting to be lost in the music. She wanted to remember her father's face as he'd played. She'd never heard anyone play like him before. Not until today.

"Please," she smiled.

Seeming to understand, Hank started the song again, and she was transported to 721B. Saturday morning pancakes. Trip planning. A large, gentle black man barely pressing the keys, and yet making them sing. A young girl dancing.

It also brought the sting of loss. Of falling asleep late, trying to stay awake for his arrival home after whatever gig he'd managed to book that week. The panic when he'd collapsed. Not being able to wake him. Shaky fingers dialing 911. Lights. Sirens. A sterile hospital room. Pitying doctors. The funeral day drizzle. Arriving at Iverson at the request of a Grandmother she never met who couldn't even bother to make it to the court date but sent a lawyer in her place.

Murphy released a sigh when the music stopped. She wiped her face of tears with the sleeve of her sweatshirt, hiding behind the coffee mug propped on her knees. Then she leaned against Hank who had pressed his shoulder to her back, hands still on the keys.

"My dad used to play that song. It was one of the last things he played before ..." Murphy trailed off. She shouldn't say anything more. She tried forcing the words to stop, but choked on them.

"What happened, Cain?" Hank pressed.

Her eyes closed. It was easier if she imagined herself alone. She wanted to tell him her story. Other than the bits and pieces she had shared with Emmaline, no one *really* knew.

"Every year, for my birthday, my dad would always bake cupcakes. He had to make them from scratch. A recipe my mom had used. She died when I was six months old, so it was just us. He wanted to keep her in my life as much as he could." Murphy traced the raised pattern on her coffee cup with her thumb. "My birthday is two days after Christmas, and dad never wanted it to get lost in the midst of the holiday craziness. He made it a point to make it special. He'd stop time if he could. He would wake up early to bake those cupcakes, and when I woke up, he would play Elton John's *Your Song* on the piano that took up almost the entire living room."

Hank, who had stopped playing the keys and turned slightly, rubbed circles in her back as she continued, the warmth of his hand surprisingly comforting. "'This is really your song, Murphy-girl,' he'd tell me, 'It was playing over the hospital intercom when you were born, and it was one of your mama's favorites'."

Murphy drew in a shaky breath. Hank's hand on her back giving her the courage to continue.

"Every year he'd tell me about how when I was born, I was the only birth in the hospital that day and even though mama had wished for a white Christmas, it didn't happen. But when I was born, it finally started snowing." Murphy chuckled. "A 'Murphy miracle' he called it. My daddy loved snow." Murphy used to see the magic in it, but not so much anymore. Not after years of being at Iverson and having to clean up the after-effects from the halls. Now it was just a haunting reminder of what used to be.

The next part of the story was the hardest to tell.

Murphy swallowed down the lump and continued,

determined the get through without falling apart. "The day before my eleventh birthday Daddy wasn't feeling so well. He had a morning gig, so he was going to have to get up earlier than normal to make sure everything was perfect for my special day." Murphy balled a hand into a fist. "I told him not to. I told him we could celebrate on another day, but he insisted. I got up to help him. He had been groggy and lightheaded the night before and so much more so that morning, but he wouldn't hear about canceling—my birthday celebration or the gig. When he collapsed —" Murphy's voice cracked. She cleared her throat. "When he collapsed and I couldn't wake him, I didn't know what to do. We didn't own a phone so I had to bang on three neighbor's doors before I woke someone up who could help. The ambulance came and took him away. He was in the hospital for three days. He never woke up."

Hank's arm came around the front of Murphy's knees and he tucked her to him. "I'm so sorry, Cain," he whispered into her hair.

Murphy wrapped her fingers around his forearm—meeting the fair hair on his arm where his sleeves were rolled up. She needed to tell him the rest. Had to tell him about Tripp and the platform and the misunderstanding. She didn't want this secret between them anymore.

She shifted to face him. "Hank—" she started.

"Yeah, Cain?" He brushed her hair from her face, letting his hand linger on her shoulder.

"Hank? Where you at, Dude?"

The twins came rushing around the corner like a late 204 to New York speeding down the track. Murphy pushed away from the piano bench, gripping her mug in front of her like a shield. She took two steps back, not able to break eye contact with Hank. Everything around her hazed away.

What had just happened? What had she been about to do? Even if she wanted to tell him the truth, she couldn't. He would react like everyone else. Why had she told him her story?

Hank turned to the twins bounding across the room, hollering something about figuring out the challenges for *Sir Siegfried's Quest*. Murphy blinked, and the spell was broken. The room came back into focus. She turned and smiled at Floyd and Lloyd.

"Do you guys need some coffee?" Murphy heard the tremble in her voice and, from the look Hank gave her, he'd heard it too.

She needed to get out. The room felt like it was closing in around her and she could no longer breathe around Hank.

"I'm going to see if there is any left," she escaped to the hallway.

Using the wall to hold her up she paused, listening to the chatter of the twins and Hank's calm voice answering them distractedly. She sucked in a deep breath trying to steady her racing heart, and with her head down shuffled back to the kitchen.

CHAPTER THIRTEEN

CHRISTMAS EVE officially marked Murphy's one-week break. She celebrated by sleeping in way too late before having coffee and muffins with the twins. Now, she was busy with dinner preparations. Per tradition, Mrs. Potts always cooked a feast for Murphy, Mr. Gruber, and any remaining students. It normally consisted of the twins and one or two stragglers, but this year it would just be the five of them. Murphy couldn't help feeling a little twinge that she didn't invite Hank to their little celebration as well. Hank *and* Eloise. She would have invited both of them she told herself.

The gravelly voice of Bing Crosby sang the low notes of Silent Night over the speakers in the mess hall as Murphy padded across the floor in her moccasin slippers, carrying a basket full of rolls hot from the oven. Setting the basket down, she surveyed the table. Going through a mental checklist, she made sure everything was perfect before Mrs. P and Mr. Gruber returned from the Christmas Eve service. They were due back any minute.

Murphy dropped two dollops of sweet cream into her

coffee. Taking a long swig, she let the drink sit on her tongue. Had she really told Hank about her father? There was no way she could now hide the fact she wasn't from his world. Which student from Iverson grew up in an apartment barely big enough for a piano? She was so stupid.

Then another memory hit. Her face warmed at the thought of Hank holding her. As much as she didn't want to admit it, she'd liked it. Really liked it.

The double doors banged open, Floyd and Lloyd appeared.

"Really, guys? Where's the fire?"

"Haha. So funny," Lloyd said

"We just didn't want to be late," Floyd added.

"And we're starving." The boys said in practically one breath.

"You guys are such weirdos. You know we're the only ones eating tonight. Plus, it isn't like you are doing anything else tonight."

Both boys slid in a chair at the table, trying—and failing—to hide a badly wrapped package behind them. Murphy couldn't keep the smile from lighting her face.

"What are you guys hiding?" she asked sweetly, putting her mug of coffee on the table.

Floyd rolled his eyes and bumped his brother. "Might as well hand it over already."

Lloyd matched his brother's eye roll and produced a bulky gift wrapped in what looked like a paper grocery bag and held together with twine. "We couldn't find any tape." Lloyd blushed.

"It's not that much of anything, really." Floyd was blushing now, too, as he plopped the gift in Murphy's grabby hands.

She was almost too scared to open it by the boys' reaction. Blushing, really? The twins didn't blush. Her curiosity was strong, and it was all she could do not to tear into the package. Carefully working at the knot, trying to not smile at the twins practically jumping out of their seat for her to move faster.

Finally, loosening the string, she peeled back the paper to reveal the most beautiful vintage leather satchel.

Murphy blinked back unexpected tears. She ran her hands over the worn leather. It was the perfect kind of soft. "You guys."

"We got your initials there on the front too. It just seemed right. You needed a new computer bag, and that one should last you a few trips around the world."

Her fingers slide over the gold ink stamped MJC. "Awe. Come here." The table was way too big to hug over, but that didn't stop Murphy. She reached as far as she could, careful not to bump her coffee, and pulled Floyd and Lloyd into a quick, half-neck squeeze, half-back pat. She sniffed, pulling the bag to her chest as everyone settled back into their chairs. "I love it. Thank you so much."

"It was nothing. We just..." Lloyd shrugged. "We thought you might like it."

She swiped the back of her hand across her face. "I love it. Do you want yours?"

Both boys responded with their own grabby hands. Murphy relented and handed over two matching Christmas bags.

Both boys fist bumped over the limited-edition Star Trek Funko Pops that she had found while shopping with Hank and Eloise. She had squealed when she saw them knowing they would be an amazing addition to their collections. She'd included a bag of Funyuns and a Red Bull for each of them as well. Still her gifts paled in comparison with theirs.

"Don't open those Funyuns in here," Murphy chided, stopping both boys mid-open. "You know Mrs. P is sure to smell them, and then we'll all be in trouble."

Both boys grumbled, but knowing Murphy was right, slipped the chips back into the gift bag and tucked them under the table.

"You guys started opening presents without us?"

They turned to see Mr. Gruber pushing through the swinging doors to the kitchen, carrying a stack of presents.

"Now, Amos, you leave them alone," Mrs. Potts scolded from in the kitchen. She appeared moments later; her own arms laden with packages.

"Of course, Carol," Mr. Gruber replied, turning to help her with the gifts.

He handed two boxes to each of the teens, who tore into them with giggles and exclamations. Dinner momentarily forgotten.

Both boys received a sweater knitted by Mrs. Potts herself. Floyd's was dark red with a gold "F" knitted on the chest. Lloyd's dark blue with a green "L". They had a good laugh when they realized they each had the other's sweater. Both instantly pulled their sweater over their head, exclaiming just how much they loved the homemade gift. Mrs. Potts blubbered and turned three shades of pink at the special attention.

Murphy also got a sweater — the same as ever year. Hers a creamy milk color. Most would think that a home-made sweater was up there with receiving underwear from your grandmother, but the twins weren't lying in their praise. Mrs. Potts' sweaters really were that great. The best kind of slouchy comfort.

The second packages were from Mr. Gruber. His gifts were always — something else. One year, Murphy got a horseshoe. They'd all had a good laugh about that gift, but Murphy still had it hanging above her doorway. With Mr. Gruber, you never knew what you were going to get.

This year it was relatively tame, and Murphy had an idea that it was because Mr. Gruber enlisted Mrs. Potts' help. For Murphy, Mr. Gruber had gotten a variety of chocolates — enough to probably last her until Easter at least (unless Emmaline found the stash. Then they'd have it gone in a weekend). For each of the boys, he had gotten a small pocketknife. Which was humorous considering Murphy was fairly certain there was no way they would ever have a need for a pocketknife.

The twins had gotten Mrs. Potts a huge batch her favorite tea in a limited-edition tea tin, which she fawned over. They gifted Mr. Gruber with thick leather gloves. Murphy thought it was sweet they had noticed his favorite pair had holes worn into them. Murphy gave Mr. Gruber the bag of hard lemon candies she had found when shopping with Hank and Eloise and paired it with fisherman's lotion for his poor hands. For Mrs. Potts she had found the cutest vintage recipe box that still had recipes in it. Mrs. Potts started crying when she opened it.

Gifts exchanged and stowed away for the moment (except for the sweaters which all recipients were currently wearing) the five turned to the feast that Mrs. Potts had prepared.

Even though Murphy had spent the last hour making sure everything was properly prepped and set out on the table, she was still amazed at the amount of food Mrs. Potts had made. There was a turkey *and* a ham which was outrageous since Murphy didn't even eat meat. But Mrs. Potts and Lloyd preferred turkey while Mr. Gruber and Floyd preferred ham, so she made both. There were two kinds of potatoes, green bean casserole—Murphy's favorite—corn, figgy pudding, rolls, and three kinds of pie.

Massive amount of food that it was, with Iverson closed the next week, there would be lots of leftovers for the teens and Mr. Gruber to pick through while Mrs. Potts visited her son-in-law and daughter in the city.

"So, Murphy, you planning on going to the Harrington's tomorrow for Christmas?" Mrs. Potts asked passing the basket of rolls around the table.

Murphy swallowed before answering, not really sure she wanted to go now that she had spilled her story. Would he treat her differently? "Hank and Eloise are going to pick me up around 10:30."

A smile lit up Mrs. Potts' face. "I'm so glad that you won't be spending Christmas morning by yourself."

"Hey! What about us?" Floyd spluttered.

Mrs. Potts waved her hand. "You boys do just fine. You were planning on not doing anything except tinker away on that video game stuff."

Both twins shrugged their shoulders. "You have a point."

Everyone laughed at the admission.

They talked more of Christmas break plans, the twins — video game creating, Mrs. Potts — her train was leaving at six in the morning and she was spending the entire week at her daughter's house, and Mr. Gruber — planning to finish reading Dostoyevsky and eating the entire bag of lemon candy Murphy got him. They ate until they could eat no more, told countless stories of Christmases before, and laughed until their sides hurt. It was well past dark when they finally started clearing the tables, all pitching in to get the work done.

When the last dish was washed and dried, Mrs. Potts pulled out a saucepan to begin making her "practically perfect peppermint hot cocoa" while Murphy started popping popcorn over the stove. The three boys sat at the table discussing which holiday movie they would play this year even though everyone already knew they would start with the classic, It's a Wonderful Life, and then move on to a traditional favorite, Elf.

Steaming chocolate and fragrant popcorn finally ready, they all piled into the media room.

Mr. Gruber and Mrs. Potts sat on one side of the black leather sectional, a bowl of popcorn between them. Murphy and the twins shared the other — with Murphy in the middle holding the bowl.

With a mug of cocoa warming her hands, the lights dimmed, and the angel's voice beginning the opening lines of the movie, Murphy looked around. Mr. Gruber was tucking a blanket across Mrs. P's lap. Murphy smiled. Mrs. Potts had been a widow for a while, and she loved that Mr. Gruber always seemed to take care of her — wanting nothing more. And Mrs. Potts always doted over Mr. Gruber as well. Theirs was the best kind of friendship.

For once, the twins were calm, not trying to make or pull any kind of joke. Well, other than randomly keeping Murphy from grabbing a handful of popcorn by ducking their hand under hers whenever she'd reach for popcorn. She finally gave up on the snack choosing instead to just drink her cocoa until, of course, she went to take a drink and discovered a piece of popcorn floating on the top. When she asked the boys about it, they feigned innocence and told Murphy to "shhh."

She felt a sort of calm fall over her looking at the people who really loved her the most in life. Emmaline was right. They simply accepted who she was, not caring that she hadn't come from money. Suddenly, it was hard for Murphy to swallow past the lump in her throat.

"You ok, Murph?" Lloyd whispered.

Murphy smiled at Lloyd, blinking the tears she knew were glistening in her eyes. She nodded and leaned her head on his shoulder.

Yes. For the first time in a long time everything felt right. She was truly and utterly ok.

CHAPTER FOURTEEN

"MERRY CHRISTMAS, EMMA," Murphy yawned.

"Merry Christmas, Murph," Emmaline had her computer propped up while she fixed her hair and expertly brushed mascara on her already popping eyelash extensions. "Just finish movie night?"

"Mm," Murphy balled her pillow under her head. "Mrs. Potts had to leave after the first movie since she's leaving so early tomorrow. Mr. Gruber followed her."

"I swear there is something going on between those two. Speaking of Christmas, have you found your gift yet?"

Murphy sat up, suddenly not feeling as tired. "What? No! How did you ... When?" she slid off the bed and stood in the middle of the room surveying it as if the gift would simply appear.

Emmaline shook her head, laughing. "I can't believe you haven't found it yet. I hid it before I left!" She nodded behind Murphy. "Desk. Top right drawer."

Murphy flung open the drawer and pulled out a smallish box wrapped in shiny silver paper and a glittering black ribbon.

"It's so beautiful I almost don't want to open it," Murphy said running her fingers over the silky ribbon.

"Oh, stop it. Open it already."

"I said almost," Murphy smiled, tugging the gift away from its wrapping. She opened the box to reveal a paperback copy of *The Great Gatsby*.

"I noticed your copy was looking a little worn," Emmaline hurriedly explained. "Plus, that looked like a pretty cool edition."

"Emma, this is great." Murphy set the paperback on her bed agreeing that whatever artist designed the cover was her new favorite. Tugging the ribbon from Fiona's mouth, she said, "Ok. Your turn."

"My turn?" Emmaline paused mid mascara swipe.

"You didn't think I'd let you fly halfway across the world at Christmastime and not hide a present in your luggage, did you?" Murphy put her hands on her hips.

Emmaline squealed and disappeared from view. Murphy giggled seeing clothes flash across the screen as her friend dug into the very bottom of her suitcase where Murphy had hidden the gift.

"It's not much."

Emmaline flew back into view the gift in her hands. She shook it close to her ear, but it gave no sound. As Murphy knew it wouldn't. Murphy watched, while biting her thumb nail. Not being able to wait any longer, Emmaline tore off the paper.

"Murphy, I love it."

"Really? I wasn't sure about the color." Murphy bit her lip.

"Shut your mouth, I love it." Emmaline wrapped the homemade deep purple scarf around her neck. Mrs. Potts had been teaching her to knit. She still wasn't great, but she could knit a large rectangle and call it a scarf. "I am totally going to wear this every day."

"I'm so glad you like it." Murphy yawned again, not able to fight it any longer.

"You have a big day planned with Tripp and family?" Emmaline asked.

Nodding, Murphy crawled back into her bed, letting Fiona curl up next to her. "Yeah, Hank and Eloise are going to pick me up around 10:30."

Emmaline shook her head.

"What?" Murphy's words were starting to slur.

"You totally have the starry look in your eyes."

"That, dear Emmaline, is simply the sleepy look in my eyes. Believe me I have no stars in my eyes." Her excuse sounded weak even to her ears.

"Sure you don't," Emmaline grinned. "I'm going to let you go to bed. Have fun tomorrow and feel free to raid my closet if you need to."

"Mmk." Murphy's eyes were already half closed, and as Emmaline said her goodbyes, Murphy realized she forgot to tell her that she had been right. She did have people who accepted her for her.

———

THE NEXT MORNING, Murphy was so glad Emmaline had given her permission to raid her closet — not like she hadn't known she could already. She dressed in black leggings, a Star Wars t-shirt, and her new slouchy sweater from Mrs. Potts, but for the life of her, she couldn't bring herself to wear her beat up Cons.

Emmaline to the rescue.

While there was at least six inches difference in height,

they wore the same shoe size. Murphy slipped her feet into a pair of black flats completing the look. The teal bottoms even matched the lettering on her t-shirt. Standing back, she observed herself in Emmaline's floor to ceiling mirror.

She smoothed out her hair, which she had used Emmaline's straightener on, and adjusted her sweater on her shoulders. She dabbed on a little of lip gloss, as fancy in the makeup department as she was willing to get.

Practically skipping down the stairs, Murphy gathered up her coat and scarf and headed to wait in the entry for her ride to the Harringtons'. When was the last time she had Christmas with family? Seven years ago? She hadn't thought of that Christmas in ages, the days after having tainted the memory. That year her father had gotten her a pair of shoes with pink sparkles and had splurged on tickets to the ballet later that month—they had never gotten to attend. By the date of the ballet, her father had been buried for over a week and she was beginning her new life at Iverson.

Not more than five minutes later, Hank pulled up to the front steps.

"Where's Eloise?" Murphy asked when Hank slid back into the car after holding the door open for her. She was a little surprised that the youngest Harrington hadn't tagged along.

Hank looked in the back seat if only just realizing that his sister hadn't ridden over with him. "She wanted to stay back. Help get everything ready."

Murphy felt a little light headed at being alone with Hank. They hadn't been alone since she had walked in on him playing piano and she had told him about her losing her dad. They'd had a moment. At least she thought she felt something. Had he? "Ready for what?"

"Ready for present opening!"

"You guys haven't opened presents yet?" Murphy felt her stomach drop. She hadn't even thought about gifts for the Harringtons. She figured she was going after all the normal present opening had happened. They hadn't known her long enough to include her.

"No, Eloise wanted to wait for you."

"But I didn't get anything—"

"Cain, stop." Hank put his hand on top of hers. Her stomach went into all kinds of butterfly fits. "You don't have to worry about gifts. We don't care about that. We just wanted you to come hang out with us. As Tripp's girlfriend, you are practically part of the family now."

"Okay," Murphy's stomach plummeted. She was *Tripp's* girlfriend. They moment at the piano was all in her head. Nothing could happen between her and Hank. What she felt at the piano must have been Hank comforting her just like he'd comfort Eloise if she were upset. But it didn't feel that way to Murphy.

If she told him she wasn't really Tripp's girl could there be something there then? Of course not. If she told the truth, not only would she be seen as a liar, but Hank would also realize what she really was. Just a Cinderella living in a closet.

There was something about the Harrington house that had a magical Christmas feel. She did notice there were more twinkle lights strung up, and she assumed that the addition of lights were in preparation for the upcoming Christmas ball.

Jarvis was already opening the door, and Murphy couldn't help but give him a hug and wish him a Merry Christmas. The older man stiffened, probably not accustomed to hugs, but patted her back, and wished her a Merry Christmas as well.

Hank steered Murphy to a part of the house she had yet to be in. The room was almost ... normal. Not what she expected from the Harrington house, but it was instantly Murphy's favorite.

There was a roaring fire in the fireplace, a Christmas tree that looked covered in family mementos of years past. Eloise and Grandpa Jack were both still in their matching Santa pajamas, sitting on the floor with backs leaning against the couch. Richard Harrington looked odd without his ever-present phone in his hand, his arm resting on the back of the couch almost around his wife. Murphy was sure his phone was stashed somewhere close—just in case of an emergency. Tabitha Harrington looked almost relaxed. She was wearing jeans and a sweater, her hair soft around her shoulders. She held a mug of coffee and she was laughing at a story her father was telling her.

"Murphy, Merry Christmas!" Tabitha greeted. Hearing her mother's greeting, Eloise jumped up and ran to Murphy pulling her to sit next to her on the floor. Grandpa Jack pushed a Santa mug full of coffee into her hands.

"Now that you're here, we can open presents!" Eloise exclaimed, grabbing a wrapped present from under the tree. "This one is for you, Hank!" She tossed the present to her brother. He caught it one handed, the other clutching his own coffee.

Laughing, he settled down next to Murphy as Eloise turned back to the pile of gifts handing everyone one before looking for one for herself.

"Here, Murphy, this one is for you."

"That one is from Tabitha and me," Richard said. He had put aside the tie from Eloise he just finished opening and leaned his elbows on his knees. Tabitha seemed to lean forward as well waiting for Murphy to open the gift.

She bit her lip, the added attention making her feel even more guilty. With an encouraging smile from Hank, Murphy ripped the present open.

A cell phone. The Harringtons had gotten her a cell phone.

"Eloise had mentioned you didn't have a phone, and we figured since you are Tripp's girlfriend, it was the least we could do," Tabitha said.

Murphy turned the box over in her hands. Her chest tightened. This was no longer about her fitting into a group of people. She was dragging the Harringtons down with her — wherever this was taking her.

"We have the plan payed up for the next six months, but we can extend that as long as you want. You don't need to worry about a thing," Richard added.

Murphy hesitated before responding, "Thank you." For the first time, she realized she was taking advantage of the Harringtons. This isn't what it was supposed to be like at all. She was just supposed to be in and out of their lives. Just to go to the brunch and get a taste of what it would be to be one of the "in" crowd. But this. This was something way deeper. How had she gotten to this place? The longer she stayed the harder it was going to be to simply fade away. This wasn't right. She felt her eyes fill with tears and she bit down hard on her lip to keep them from falling. She was glad everyone had shifted their attention to Grandpa Jack who just opened a mega pack of silly string from Hank. Grandpa Jack proceeded to pop the cap off the can, and Tabitha was nervously telling her father to put it away.

Murphy could feel her breathing go shallow. They were all here. All the Harringtons plus Grandpa Jack. She could tell them who she really was. The phone felt like a brick in her hand. A phone. They had gotten her a phone — and a sparkly phone case too. Thirteen-year-old Murphy would have been over the moon, but seventeen-year-old Murphy just felt like a fake. She bit her bottom lip. Everyone was so happy now. Telling them today would ruin their Christmas. Tabitha was actually smiling. She couldn't do that to them. She could wait until later.

"You okay?" Hank whispered.

Murphy blinked fast, clearing her eyes of the pesky emotion. She nodded at him, offering him a smile.

His eyes bored hers, searching. Her breath hitched. She tried to remind herself that there could be nothing there. Hank was a nice guy. After she told him her story, he would know Christmas was hard for her and wanted to make sure she was okay.

Their eyes held each other a minute more before Hank gave her shoulder a supporting squeeze and let his hand drop. Murphy had to get her emotions in check.

Screams and protesting erupted when Grandpa Jack let neon streams of silly string fly spraying anyone who dared try to move away. Murphy giggled, feeling the release of emotion. Grandpa Jack rescuing her from the climbing tension.

The day was filled with food, laughter, and at least four more surprise silly string attacks from Grandpa Jack, including much to the nurse on duty's dismay, one in Tripp's room.

When all the paper and ribbon and tinsel settled, Murphy had received the phone from Richard and Tabitha and a bright pink and glittery case for said phone from Eloise. Grandpa Jack had thrown in a deck of cards and her very own pipe — which she would have to hide at the risk of expulsion. She also opened several gifts from Tripp. Eloise and Tabitha insisted they were stashed away in Tripp's room there at home, but Murphy had a sneaking suspicion the girls had gone on a shopping spree. None of clothes she received looked anything like Claire's style.

Claire. Tripp's real girlfriend. Murphy felt like the world's biggest shumck.

Standing in the hallway, she gathered her coat and scarf from Jarvis. Hank had jogged to his car to get it warmed up before the two-minute drive back to Iverson.

"Murphy?"

Murphy turned to see Tabitha coming up the hall. She stiffened when Tabitha put her arms around her. "Thank you."

"F-for what?" Murphy stammered.

The older woman stepped back, hands still on Murphy's shoulders. "You, you aren't like the other girls Tripp has brought around." Of course, there would be other girls. Murphy didn't know why that sounded like such a shock. Tripp had had many different girlfriends over the years before Claire. Even he and Claire had only been going out for a few weeks at best. Murphy hadn't thought that he would have brought them home to meet his family. "You're so different. Refreshing. And Eloise and Hank love you."

Murphy ducked her head. They loved her? She felt her deceit like it was written on her forehead. If only they could read it and save her the pain of breaking the news to them. Tabitha pulled her back into a hug.

"I wish it would just hurry up and snow already," Hank came in from outside stomping his feet. "I was really hoping for a white Christmas. What gives?" He looked up catching a glimpse of his mother hugging Murphy. His eyebrows shot up. Murphy raised her hands just as perplexed as he was.

"I should let you get home. Hank, make sure she gets back safely." Tabitha patted Murphy's shoulder and left.

"That was strange." Hank said. "What just happened?"

"I have no idea," Murphy said, tugging her coat on. She tried to pick up her bags, but Hank took them from her, following her out to the car. Murphy was suddenly ready to be back at Iverson. Curled under her blanket. Fiona curled next to her. Fiona. Tripp's cat. She inwardly groaned. What a hole had she dug for herself. No this wasn't a hole, this was an entire abyss.

"You're awfully quiet tonight, Cain."

Murphy sucked in a deep breath. If she was brave, she would tell Hank the truth now. She would lay everything bare. She would leave the gifts in his car when he dropped her off. The gifts that were meant for someone else. The guilt was eating her insides.

But she wasn't brave. Her admission would crush them, and she couldn't do that to them. Didn't want to do that to them.

"I'm just kind of tired." Which wasn't a lie. It just wasn't the full truth. Christmas always seemed to wear Murphy out. It was always hard. She started remembering and the remembering brought the pain of what had been and what would never be. It brought the pain of what had come next.

She picked at the fraying edge of her jacket while watching the dark landscape fly by in the silence — kind of what she felt like the break was doing. Flying by so fast and so dark she couldn't get a grasp on life. Couldn't figure out what she needed to do.

That wasn't true. She knew what she needed to do. But

if she knew, then why wasn't she acting on it. Why were the words getting stuck every time she tried to confess?

By the time Hank pulled the car up Iverson's drive, Murphy felt like she was suffocating. She had already unwrapped her scarf and had it twisted into knots her lap.

She unbuckled as soon as Hank parked the car, hand already on the door handle. She opened the door grabbing the couple of gift bags that were on the floor in front of her. She was going to have to take the time to get the ones out of the back as well.

"Hey, Cain, what's the rush?" Hank tugged her back into the car.

Murphy sucked in her bottom lip. Her heart stilled as her eyes dropped to a gift wrapped in brown paper on his lap.

"I was going to give this to you earlier but thought with all the hubbub I'd wait."

Her hand shook a little as she took the gift from him.

"Really, if I could get you anything, I'd jet you off to a destination, but thought you might rather travel with Tripp once he wakes up."

I'd rather travel with you. The realization shocked her with its honesty.

Hank prattled on as if he was actually nervous. "But I saw this at the bookstore last week and thought that it might be perfect."

Murphy let the wrapping fall away revealing a leather-bound journal. "A travel journal?"

"A travel journal. That way once you start traveling if you can't take your big map with you, you can record all your destinations here."

While she was appreciative of the phone and phone case that came from the Harringtons and the gifts that were wrapped supposedly from Tripp, this gift, a gift from the heart, meant so much more.

"Hank." His name was a whisper as she flipped through the pages. Pages waiting to be filled by her travels.

"Anyways. I saw it and thought you needed it." Hank pushed a hand through his hair.

"It's perfect. Thank you," Murphy turned in her seat. Still one foot out the door. She couldn't bring herself to leave.

Hank lifted his hand toward Murphy but before he touched her curled his hand into a fist. He blew out a nervous laugh, bounced his fist on the steering wheel. "I'd better let you get going."

Murphy sat there, frozen though not from the cold. Was it possible that Hank—

No, she wouldn't even let her mind go there. But maybe ... possibly ... could Hank have feelings for her? The thought thrilled and terrified her. She was Tripp's girlfriend. Fake girlfriend. She was supposed to care about him. Was supposed to be there for him so that when he woke up he'd see what a great fit she was for him. That he'd see her.

But the reality of it was that this sweet boy in front of her saw her better than she saw herself. Hank was stealing her heart all while Tripp was sleeping.

"Yeah," Murphy ducked her head, tucked a piece of hair behind her ear. What was she thinking? She had to get out of here. Her insides felt like molten lava. She was freezing and burning up all at the same time.

With one final look at Hank, she slipped from the car, and grabbed her bags from the back.

"Hey, Cain," Hank called before the door closed all the way.

"Yes?" Her heart was racing. Was this it? Was he going to profess his undying love?

Hank looked at her. That one gaze shooting icy hot sparks through her. She sucked in a breath, holding it. This *was* it. He was going to—

"The Christmas bash is tomorrow. I just wanted to see if you made your mind up about coming."

—Remind her about the party.

Her lungs deflated. She had completely read that wrong. Maybe he didn't feel for her what she was feeling for him. Or maybe she was just projecting her feelings for Tripp onto Hank. Yes, that's what was happening. She was still in love with Tripp.

"I mean I know that you said you'd think about it, but Eloise is dying for you to come and save her the boredom. And Mother would really like you to be there—she's already set your place. It's important to her, especially since everything with Tripp..."

Murphy smiled. "Of course, I'll be there."

"Great. I'll see you tomorrow."

She let the door close and dashed up the steps and into the warmth of Iverson.

This was ridiculous. *She* was being ridiculous. Letting the bags fall to the floor, Murphy leaned against the wall. She needed to get her feelings under control. She hit her head on the wall, as if that could actually drive thoughts of Hank and her feelings for him from her mind.

Groaning she looked at the packages at her feet. She wasn't really sure what she was going to do with them since she didn't feel like she should keep them. Maybe it would be better to just put them in Claire's room. That's who these gifts were meant for anyway.

· · ·

TEXT NOTIFICATIONS

From Eloise Harrington (09:37 PM)

Am I your very first text? Like ever?

From Murphy Cain (09:41 PM)

Ever ever :)

From Eloise Harrington (09:42)

So cool.

From Hank Harrington (09:45 PM)

Welcome to the land of not the old fashioned!

From Murphy Cain (09:47 PM)

Haha

From Hank Harrington (09:52 PM)

:)

CHAPTER FIFTEEN

"THIS HAD BETTER BE GOOD," Emmaline's words slurred together. She flipped on the lamp at the same time she pushed up her sleep mask, groaning and shooting the lamp a dirty look for the offensive bright light.

Murphy was pacing back and forth in her room. She stopped and bent over the computer when she heard her friend's spluttering. "Oh good. You're awake."

She felt bad for video calling Emmaline so late, or early, but this seemed like a good enough reason. It was an emergency.

Emmaline pushed her comforter off and sat up, pulling her computer to her knees. "Well, I am now. What's going on? I think you're starting to resemble Fiona there."

"What?" Murphy looked behind her to the puff of fur that was pacing back and forth behind her.

"And what in the world are those?" Emmaline pointed a finger at the pile of gifts that Murphy had tossed on the bed.

Murphy turned and looked as if there was a pack of spiders behind her ready to pounce. "Gifts," she said. "From the Harringtons. Emmaline. Focus."

Her friend blinked, a slow grin spreading on her face. She propped her chin on her hand. "I'm totally focused."

"Right. Emmaline, I have a problem." Murphy was back to pacing and chewing her thumbnail.

"Do tell," Emmaline yawned.

Murphy stopped her back and forth and put her face directly on the screen. "Emma, I'm serious here!"

"Murph, first, no more of that ridiculous pacing. You're giving me a headache. Second, you need to explain what in the world is going on. I can't fix the problem until I hear what it is." Emmaline took a swig of a Diet Coke that was sitting on her nightstand. Apparently, it was warm, or flat, because she instantly spit it back into the can.

"The Christmas party thing," Murphy spit out in a single breath.

"The Harrington's Christmas Ball?"

Murphy nodded her head up and down feeling like a bobble head. She sucked in air feeling like she couldn't get enough.

"So, what about it?"

"It's kind of tomorrow. Tonight? I don't even know what day it is," Murphy ran her fingers through her hair.

"That's your problem?" Emmaline deadpanned. "Are you sure your tizzy isn't about Hank?"

"Hank? Why would it be about Hank?"

"Um, because you so like him!"

Murphy paused. "No. It's totally about the party. Ball. Whatever. I have no idea what in the world I'm supposed to do at one of these things. This is not my thing. I don't even think I have anything to wear." Murphy was back to pacing, alternating between wringing her hands and biting her thumbnail. "Besides what if someone from school sees me there? They are definitely going to know that I'm not

Tripp's girlfriend." A sickening thought struck Murphy. "Emmaline, what if Claire shows up?"

"Is that all?" Emmaline fell back against her pillows.

"Is that all?" Murphy squeaked. "I can't go to a party and be introduced to everyone as Tripp's girlfriend. Emma, I'm not Tripp's girlfriend!"

Emmaline looked at Murphy incredulously, her coke can paused half way back to the nightstand.

Murphy waved a hand toward her computer. "I know, I know. You can skip the 'I told you so.'"

"Ok, well, now that we've got that out of the way, I have a simple solution. You're going to go to the party."

"Wait? What?"

Emmaline, the one that had been dead set against her playing girlfriend since the very beginning. Only two days ago she wasn't talking to Murphy because of it. And now she was what? Telling her to embrace it?

"Oh, it's too early for this." Emmaline rolled her eyes and pushed herself out of her bed. Balancing her laptop in front of her with one hand, she crossed the room and took a Diet Coke from the mini fridge. Popping it open, she took a long, drawn-out swig. "Don't looked so shocked, Murph. The simple fact is, you can't back out of this right now."

"Why not? This seems like the perfect time to back out of this."

"And to answer your Claire question," Emmaline said ignoring the question. "I know for a fact she's not going to be at the party. My stuck-up cousin didn't want to leave the beach and her new Cabana boy."

"Cabana boy? Clarie's cheating?"

"Does that really surprise you? It's not like she's trying to hide it. Look," Emmaline pulled up photos on her phone that Claire had posted online. Photo after photo of her in barely-there bikinis draped over a tanned boy with a body that could give anyone in Hollywood a run for their money.

Claire cheating. That's why she hadn't tried to contact Tripp. Murphy felt panic settle in her stomach as she started to consider going to the party. She didn't do well in crowds. She was awkward and not eloquent and definitely not the high-class girl from Iverson the Harringtons expected. But maybe that wasn't a bad thing. She glanced at the shiny cell phone they'd gifted her. Remembered Tabitha's hug. They seemed to like her... "You're the one who told me I should tell them in the first place."

"I know, but Murphy, do it tomorrow or the next day. Play the heartbroken girlfriend who can't take a half-dead boyfriend anymore.

"The point of the matter is, if you tell them now, it'll be all anyone can talk about, and Mistress Hyde will find out. This is the worst possible time to back out. You took gifts from them—"

"I'll give them back. I wasn't planning on keeping them anyway."

"Murphy, this is what you wanted," she reminded her. "You wanted to be part of the in crowd. Wanted to show everyone you belonged."

Murphy fell back against her bed, completely deflated. "I know, but I take it back. I don't think I can do this."

Emmaline gave her a half-hearted smile. "Well, we are going to embrace it now, and you are going to have the time of your life at that party."

"I don't know."

"You have to because otherwise what is Ralph going to do?"

"Ralph? Like Ralph from your dream team Ralph?"

Murphy was so confused. What did he have to do with if she went to the party or not?

Emmaline pushed out a breath. "I guess this is as good time as any to tell you." She set her computer on her dresser and stood back, hands on hips.

Murphy tilted her head at the computer, one eye opened. "Tell me what?"

"I was going to surprise you tomorrow, but what the heck."

"Emmaline!" Murphy had grabbed either side of her computer as if this would compel her friend to spit it out. "What?"

Her friend was enjoying the suspense, mouth curled up in a cat-like smile partially hidden behind her fists. Murphy focused on Emmaline, the anticipation coiling around her.

"Ralph and his team will be there tomorrow afternoon to help you get ready." The admission finally spilled from Emmaline, grin so big it could have lit the Eiffel Tower.

"The entire team?"

Ralph Levine and his stylists were Emmaline's beauty team. Whenever her father had some big function in the city, Emmaline would visit Ralph's studio first. There had been only one time he had made the trip to Iverson. It was the end of Junior year for the spring fling dance—not that Murphy had gone. Well, hadn't gone as a student. Since it wasn't considered academia, Murphy wasn't allowed to go. Instead, she'd donned the black and white uniform of a server.

"Yes. I called him last week and set it up."

Murphy blinked back the tears welling up. Last week after she told her about the invitation. When they weren't on the best of speaking terms. "Oh, Emma. You are amazing, but I still don't have anything to wear."

"I thought of that too." She rolled her eyes. "Your dress is arriving..." Emmaline picked up her phone and after a few taps flipped the phone so Murphy could see. "Right on time."

It took a minute for the image to focus. It was backwards, but it looked like a train schedule and some shipping number. Murphy squinted and tilted her head as if that would help clear and revert the image. "It's backwards." She finally gave up.

Emmaline turned the phone back to her. "Right. Your dress is arriving on the noon train from New York. I had it shipped express. I hope you don't mind that I picked it out."

"But ... how am I supposed to get it? Ralph is coming at noon." Murphy scanned the train schedules from memory. There was literally no way to meet the noon train and be at Iverson for Ralph. And she'd have to get a ride to the station from the twins anyway. Emmaline interrupted her thoughts.

"Already took care of it. I bribed the twins with a month's supply of Funyuns and Red Bull. They are all in to pick up your dress."

Maybe it was because it was so late. Maybe it was from all the excitement and pent up energy of the day, but Murphy's head was spinning as if she was on a merry-go-round. She didn't have to live on the same floor as them or have to have multibillionaire parents, but her people loved her for being herself. She shook her head back and forth. "Emmaline, I don't know how I could ever repay you."

Emmaline waved her hand. "Consider it an early birthday present."

Murphy didn't do anything to stop the tears from overflowing now. "Thank you so much," she choked out.

"Just call me your fairy godmother." Emmaline waved an invisible wand. "Bibbity bobbiddy boo."

"I love you." Murphy laughed through her tears. "You truly are the best, and I'm sorry I woke you up so early."

"What are friends for?" Emmaline's shoulders lifted in a shrug. "Now, Murph. Get a good night's sleep and go knock 'em dead."

CHAPTER SIXTEEN

EVEN THOUGH EMMALINE had taken care of quite literally everything, exhaustion didn't keep the worried thoughts or excitement at bay long enough for Murphy to sleep well. At the end of the night she probably had slept only two hours. And even those were rough, filled with tossing and turning.

She wasn't fully asleep when a blaring siren started going off in her ear. She bolted up scrambling for the source of the sound.

Finally finding the phone encased in the sparkly pink case, she swiped to answer and held the phone up to her ear making a mental note that if she was going to keep the phone, the first thing she needed to do was change the terrible ring tone.

"Hello?" She barely got out around the sleep in her voice.

"Are you still sleeping? Sleepyhead." Eloise's giggled.

Murphy grabbed the digital clock from her windowsill, squinting to read the numbers displayed. 9:15. She inwardly groaned.

"I—" Murphy heard a protest from Hank and could practically see Eloise rolling her eyes with her next statement.

"Hank and I," she amended. "Left you a gift in the front hallway on that table thing."

Murphy pushed her comforter to the bottom of the bed, earning her an irritated meow from Fiona. She gave the cat an apologetic scratch behind the ears, which seemed to satisfy her back to sleep. "What is it?"

"Just go get it."

Winding her way through the kitchen, dining hall, down the hallway, and into the foyer she spotted something sitting on the table. It was a paper bag with a bakery logo and cup of coffee. The scent of the coffee already tickling her senses. A peek in the bag confirmed what she hoped. Blueberry scone. Her stomach growled.

"Did you find it?" Eloise asked.

"I found it." Murphy smiled. "Thank you, guys. You should have stayed."

"We had to get home. We snuck out early knowing that mother wouldn't have any good food in the house this morning. Saving it all for tonight, and if we tried to break into the kitchen, she would probably have a stroke. We all go hungry on party days."

Murphy chuckled. "Thanks for thinking of me."

"You bet. Hank said something about most the staff there being on break this week, so we didn't want you going hungry either."

She felt her stomach drop. That staff included her. She squared her shoulders. Nope, today she wasn't going to feel bad about having fun. After getting off the phone with Emmaline the night before, Murphy had decided that, at least for today, she was going to fully embrace being on the in-crowd. She wasn't going to be pulled or swayed by past decisions. She would own the role of Tripp's girlfriend. And she refused to think of "what-ifs" with Hank.

"That was sweet," she said. She took the gifts and turned to go back to her room. "I'll see you later, okay?"

"Okay. Hank said he'd be around about five to pick you up. Unless you'd like to come over earlier to get ready here?" Murphy could hear the hopefulness in Eloise's suggestion. "Mother has a team coming in to make sure we are perfect."

"I actually have a team coming here in a few hours to help me get ready." Murphy had never felt so *extra* as she did in that moment. She was positively giddy.

"No worries. We'll see you in a bit!"

The scone was still warm. Not bothering with a plate or fork, Murphy sunk her teeth into the pastry. Her eyes slid closed. This was the best scone she'd had in her entire life. It practically melted in her mouth. Frowning, she looked at the logo on the bag. This couldn't have come from Ash Hollow. Murphy would have been at least twenty pounds heavier if scones like this existed in their little town. Laughing, she shook her head. They had driven two towns over. For scones like this, Murphy would have, too.

After inhaling the scone and coffee, Murphy jumped in the shower. She made sure to pile her hair on top of her head under a shower cap with strict instructions from Emmaline not to get it wet. Dressed in her most comfy, holey sweatpants and oversized Harry Potter t-shirt, she made her way upstairs to see if the twins were awake yet. Plans of a quiet morning reading forgotten. She couldn't concentrate on a story even if she tried. After three rounds of the new and improved Sir Siegfried, Floyd announced it was time for Murphy to be transformed into a real princess. And time for them to head to the station to pick up her dress like the peasants they were. Murphy rolled her eyes. They would never let her live this down. Ever.

As the twins drove down the drive, a white van following a bright red mini cooper drove up the lane. Murphy's stomach was in knots, making her regret the scone and coffee earlier, no matter how amazing it had been.

She watched Ralph unfold himself out of the small car, recognizing him from the time he'd come to help Emmaline, and wondered why a man that tall would purchase a car that small. Another younger man and two girls tumbled from the van. Ralph stood back, hands on hips, leaned back to look all the way up at Iverson's tall pillars. Murphy stepped forward, thinking that she should see if they needed any help. The three that had been riding in the van were now pulling stuff out of the back and stacking it on the ground.

"Ah, hello." Ralph had spotted her.

"Hello. Do they need help with that?" Murphy motioned to the three struggling with pulling a large box out of the back of the van. She couldn't imagine what it might hold.

Ralph looked behind him as if expecting to see something other than his team unloading the van. "Oh no, they are fine." He stepped up to where Murphy was standing, sticking his hand out toward Murphy. "I'm Ralph Levine."

Murphy tentatively took his hand, not missing the concerned up and down that Ralph was giving her. "I'm Murphy Cain."

"Mm, yes, I was afraid that you might say that." He turned to the three who were just closing the van doors.

"Right this way, chaps! Ms. Murphy, where would you like to set up? Your room perhaps?"

"The kitchen would be better. This way." Murphy turned to lead them inside before Ralph could see her bright red face. Maybe she should have just used Emmaline's room, but then again Ralph had been in Emmaline's room before so that could have been just as suspicious.

He didn't comment on having to set up in the kitchen. Calling out commands to Jefferson, Madison, and Tara, he moved to man-in-charge. Murphy stood in the middle of the kitchen waiting for instructions. Everything moved around her in motion and she felt completely still.

Madison was the one who finally tossed a robe at Murphy telling her to change into it. It was the silkiest thing Murphy had ever felt. Once changed, Madison plopped her into a chair, both hands and feet soaking in tubs filled with some milky liquid that smelled of roses.

Tara started tugging at her hair as Madison returned. She began by dipping something out of a bowl and spreading it on Murphy's face. Murphy closed her eyes and let them work their magic.

"Excuse me, Miss Cain."

Someone was shaking her shoulder. Murphy popped up. Ugh. She had fallen asleep. She reached up to wipe her mouth. Horrors of all horrors she was actually drooling. "I am so sorry." She spluttered an apology.

Madison, or was it Tara, smiled. "No worries, Miss. We just needed you to sit up a little for this next part."

Murphy sat up tall in the chair. At some point, Madison and Tara had transformed her hands and feet into soft, dainty things. He nails were expertly painted a deep, practically black, navy color. Murphy absolutely loved it, only slightly concerned that she had slept through both a manicure and pedicure.

Ralph was leaning against the counter an espresso cup clutched between two fingers. Murphy wasn't sure why everyone sang his praises as thus far he had just barked out instructions and sipped on espresso from a machine he produced from somewhere. Once Madison and Tara were finished with her hands and toes and exfoliating and moisturizing her face, Ralph pushed off the counter and moved across the kitchen like a man on a mission.

He took position behind Murphy, who was now sitting straight with nerves, and began doing what he did best. Bark out orders. Only this time there was brushing, snipping, tugging, and pulling at Murphy's hair. She was really glad she wasn't tender headed.

Murphy's hair was in ridiculously large rollers when Jefferson appeared carrying a light in one hand and a small table in the other. He set them on either side of Murphy.

Ralph went back to sipping on espresso, Tara (Madison?) stood in front of Murphy holding a makeup compact like an artist board.

She hadn't realized how long getting ready for an event actually took. She was surprised to see that over four hours had lapsed. At some point a garment bag had appeared and was now hanging from one of the cabinets. Curiosity pulled at Murphy, but she stayed rooted to the chair while the team finished up.

Floyd strutted across the kitchen to the refrigerator ignoring the protests of Ralph. He popped a piece of leftover turkey in his mouth, letting the fridge close behind him. Then he proceeded to take his phone out of his back pocket and snapped a picture of Murphy.

"No. No! No photos until the completed masterpiece," Ralph protested jumping between Floyd and Murphy.

"Ok, ok," Floyd lifted his hand in surrender, winking at Murphy as he left the kitchen for safety.

Ralph muttered something in French before looking at Murphy, down to his watch, and back at Murphy. "We will finish your hair and then when will help you dress." He clapped his hands.

Help her dress? Murphy bit the inside of her lip to keep from protesting. *It is fine. It is fine. It is fine.*

Thirty minutes later, Murphy stood at the top of the stairs out of sight of those waiting below. Ralph had insisted on a grand entrance. Murphy would rather have not, she was still fuming a little that they had cut her out of her tee shirt to save her hair, but Ralph had insisted. The thought of a grand entrance was sending her nerves into overdrive, vibrating through her. She took another glance at herself in the floor to ceiling mirror leaning against the upstairs wall.

She could hardly believe the transformation. She understood the magic of Ralph and his team now. Her hair, usually untamable, fell in soft waves around her face, only a few pieces from one side pulled up and clipped with a diamond studded barrette. Her makeup somehow made her freckles stand out, but instead of taking away from the overall effect, they enhanced everything. She had never before worn lash extensions, but she loved the way they framed her eyes making them look so much bigger. There were four different eye shadows dusting her lids giving her a perfect smoky eye against her cocoa skin.

When Emmaline said that her dress had been express shipped, she hadn't mentioned that it was from France. The note from Emmaline said that it was an up and coming designer that she had met and fallen in love with. When she saw this particular dress and Murphy had mentioned the ball, everything clicked. Being exactly Murphy's size had cemented the plan in Emmaline's head.

The dress was the most gorgeous, deep hunter green color Murphy had ever seen. It sat slightly off her shoulders and hugged her torso before dancing into a heap at her feet. The only thing Murphy hadn't been sure about were the impossibly high, delicate, gold strappy heels that Jefferson had pulled out of the box accompanying the dress. Murphy felt like she was wobbling on the edge of the highest tower at Iverson, but Ralph would hear none of her excuses. She somehow managed to climb the back stairs and make her way down the hallway to wait for Ralph's signal for her to "float down the stairs" (Ralph's words, not hers).

"I give you, Ms. Murphy Cain," Ralph practically shouted from the bottom of the stairs. That apparently was her cue.

Taking one tentative step after another, trying her hardest not to wobble at every movement, Murphy made her way down the stairs. If it wasn't for the Christmas lights and greenery wrapped around the banister, Murphy would have clutched it like a lifeline. Her gaze moved to the landing where she saw the rest of the team huddled in the corner with giddy smiles on their faces. Floyd and Lloyd both had their camera's out. From Emmaline's demand that he 'hold the phone higher', Murphy guessed Floyd had video called her in for the big reveal. Lloyd's phone kept flashing, blinding Murphy and causing Ralph to mutter curses under his breath. Murphy guessed he was three clicks away from jerking the phone out of Lloyd's hands.

It wasn't until she saw Hank that she'd realized she had been holding her breath. She breathed out. There seemed to be an invisible cord attaching her together with Hank.

You're supposed to be thinking of Tripp. You're supposed to be his girl. You can't be thinking of Hank like this. Oh, wow, this is so messed up.

But it was *Hank* who was there, and in a tuxedo no less. He looked *good* waiting at the bottom of the stairs, the beginnings of a grin tugging the corners of his mouth upward. Murphy was sure the sight of him in a tux would never get old.

She had made it a little more than halfway down the stairs before she felt herself slipping. She took one step a little too fast and tried to keep from falling by taking the next two steps at a hop. Which was the wrong choice since the hop caused her heel to catch the inside of her dress. She heard gasps from both Ralph and Emmaline on Floyd's phone. She felt herself tipping forward and squeezed her eyes closed ready to fall the next four stairs to the bottom.

The crash never came. Instead of falling, Hank had somehow managed to grab her before she hit the ground. Her face pressed up against his shoulder, his arms wrapped around her. Safe. She could hear Ralph protesting about rubbing her makeup off, and someone said something about making sure there were no tears in her dress, but it all became white noise. Murphy was certain she never wanted to move from her current spot.

"You good, Cain?" Hank's breath tickled her ear sending shivers down her spine and stealing her ability to speak.

She nodded against his shoulder, causing more spluttering from Ralph. She straightened, ready to continue her walk down the stairs even if she had to have an awkward death grip on the railing next to her. But instead of moving aside and letting her risk falling again, Hank put his arm around her waist, letting her lean on him for the remaining steps.

Ralph stepped up to refresh her hair from the fall as Tara touched up her makeup.

"Oh, I got makeup on you," Murphy brushed at the spot on Hank's once-pristine, black jacket.

"Apparently, that isn't a problem," Hank replied as Ralph rubbed at the spot with some sponge immediately soaking up the makeup spot.

Madison draped a fur wrap over Murphy's shoulders and slipped a clutch into her hand. With well-wishes offered by everyone inside, Hank and Murphy stepped outside into the cold.

"Your carriage awaits, Madam Cain." Hank chuckled, still assisting Murphy down the steps, muttering something about how he remembered the first time they met and there was no way he was letting her attempt stairs in those heels.

As Murphy slipped inside Hank's already warm car, she just prayed that the night wouldn't end how Cinderella's had.

CHAPTER SEVENTEEN

EVEN THOUGH MURPHY had been to the Harrington house multiple times over the past two weeks, there was something about this night that felt more magical. Maybe it was because she had decided to completely embrace her role—even if it was only going to be for tonight. Tonight would be the last night. For real this time.

As soon as they walked in the door, Hank shot Murphy an apologetic look as he was swept away by his mother who was prattling on about Grandpa Jack still being in house slippers and pajama pants. Murphy found herself standing in the calm before the storm. She could hear the lifeblood of the party, the hired help, streaming through the halls, putting last touches on the decorations.

She found herself making her way to Tripp's room walking on her tiptoes to keep from wobbling so much. The dark silence was comforting. Plopping down in a chair only thinking it was a bad idea in her dress after the fact, Murphy heaved a heavy sigh.

Tonight, Tripp sported a bright red Santa hat, which Murphy was sure was courtesy of Grandpa Jack, or maybe

Hank. Either way, it brought a smile to her face. Leaning over, doing her best not to completely crumple her dress, she straightened the hat on his head.

The door clicked opened almost causing Murphy to fall completely on the bed. Emmaline would never forgive her if she ruined the dress *before* the party. Grandpa Jack came tumbling in, fingers tangled in the strings of his bowtie at his neck.

"This confounded thing," he muttered stepping into the ring of light the lamp close to Tripp's bed gave off. Heaving a sigh, he fell into the seat next to Murphy. "I give up. I think Tabitha will have my head, but I cannot get this thing tied right. Is the open neck thing a look?"

Murphy swallowed a giggle. "Come here." Straightening, she reached over and expertly tied the bow tie, fingers remembering from when she would fix her father's tie. He, much like Grandpa Jack, was hopeless when it came to tying bow ties. "What happened to Hank?"

"Oh, there was a catering emergency that Tabitha couldn't deal with. Mmh, don't that beat all," Grandpa Jack said, looking down and cross-eyed as Murphy finished. "Where'd you learn how to tie a tie like that?"

"My father was a piano player." Murphy tugged on each ends of the tie and gave it a final pat. "And he was pretty hopeless at tying his ties for formal performances."

"Does he still play?" Grandpa Jack asked slumping down in his chair.

Murphy cleared the lump from her throat. "No. He died seven years ago." *Almost to the day*, she left off.

Grandpa Jack turned bright red and stammered through an apology, patting her arm.

"You look especially dashing tonight," Murphy quickly changed the subject.

"Thank you. I can clean up pretty good when the occasion calls for it. You look exquisite. Do you think you could save a dance for an old fart like me?"

Dancing? There was going to be dancing at this thing? Murphy swallowed before telling Grandpa Jack he could have all the dances he wanted. Maybe if she danced with him, she wouldn't be tripping over her feet all night.

"There you are."

Both Murphy and Grandpa Jack looked up as Hank came into the room.

"Sorry, Grandpa Jack, to leave you like that. The caterer brought white snapper instead of red and apparently mother thought it was unacceptable. It's all worked out now." He came to a stop next to the chairs, hands in his pockets. "Your girl looks stunning tonight, eh brother?" Hank raised his eyebrows at his brother's silence. "I know my brother's being a little bit of a jerk, but I know he'd totally agree with me if he would just wake his stubborn butt up."

Murphy felt her face warm and hoped the light was dim enough to hide the reddening of her face.

"You got that right, son. Beautiful inside and out plus she's an expert at tying this ridiculous contraption." Wrinkled fingers tugged at the would-be noose around his neck.

Hank winced. "Thanks for saving my bacon, Murphy. Mother would probably have a stroke if Grandpa Jack came to dinner with no tie." He glanced at his watch. "Speaking of, we need to start heading that way."

"Oh, good. I'm starved." Grandpa Jack stood up, hands on his belly.

Murphy stood up and made it two steps before she felt her ankle roll. Hank reached out, steading her. Standing up, she tugged her dress at the bodice, making sure everything was where it should be. "Seriously, these shoes!" Why, with all the shoe possibilities, did Emmaline have to choose five-inch heels?

Hank bent over and pulled up the hem of her dress.

"What are you doing?" Murphy asked, steading herself on his back as he tugged off first one gold heel followed by the other. The wood floor was ice on her bare feet, but it was nothing to the heat she felt from his hand on her ankles. He stood up, breaking the contact, heels dangling from his fingers.

"These are not shoes, Cain, they're stilts. Why do you women insist on wearing them?" He held them at eye level as if they were about to jump off his finger and stab him in the eye.

Murphy crossed her arms over her chest. "Give me back my shoes."

Hank was already shaking his head. "Oh, no. Cain, if I give these things back you're either going to hurt yourself or someone else."

"I can't go out there barefoot." Murphy tried reaching for the shoes, but Hank held them out of her reach before tossing them across the room.

"Sure, you can," he shrugged. "That dress is long enough no one will ever know. The plus side being that you won't fall flat on your face. So really, I'm like your knight in shining armor."

Murphy shook her head as she took Hank's offered arm.

"Come, m'lady, dinner awaits."

———

AT SOME POINT, the Harrington's dining hall had been transformed into a Christmas wonderland. Murphy had to keep her mouth from dropping open at the sight of the thirty-foot tree stretching from the floor to the ceiling. The entire tree twinkling from the thousands of strands of lights hung from the branches. She felt like she had just stepped into Hogwarts at Christmas.

Unlike the morning of the awkward brunch, the people to chair ratio was perfect. Murphy noticed even the chairs from around the outside of the room had been brought to the table. For a fleeting moment, Murphy's stomach clenched. Would someone from school be here? Would they recognize her? She quickly scanned the faces of the people in the room, racking her brain for memories of anyone saying anything in the past few weeks about going to this particular party. Her stomach unwound itself when she didn't immediately notice anyone she knew.

Hank led Murphy to her seat, hand at the small of her back, shooting sparks up her spine. Murphy was seated between an older woman wearing a tiara — was she a princess? Queen? Or did she just like to be that fancy — and Grandpa Jack who shot her a wide grin when Hank pushed her chair in and disappeared to find his seat.

"I'm really glad you're sitting next to me," Grandpa Jack leaned in, whispering to Murphy. "There are three forks next to my plate, as many spoons, and two knives. I'm not sure which is for which."

She only just noticed the number of silverwares. Three goblets — one filled with ice water, condensation already forming on the outside of the glass. She had started an etiquette class when she first arrived Iverson that went over which spoon to use for which course, but once she became a ward of the school, it was academic classes only. She thought she remembered the order of things — at least enough to make it through dinner. Hopefully enough to make it through dinner. She gave Grandpa Jack what she thought was more of a smile than a grimace, but she wasn't sure.

Grandpa Jack opened his mouth to say something else but was cut off by the ringing of a bell. The buzz of the room quieted down, and Murphy heard instrumental Christmas music playing over hidden speakers. Those that were still huddled around chit-chatting found their places as servers came out carrying the first dish.

"So, you're the young Harrington's love interest?"

Murphy almost choked on her salad when the question came from the "queen" next to her. Murphy still wasn't sure what her title was, but she most definitely seemed like a snooty queen type. She finished her bite before smiling, "Yes, Ma'am."

The queen sniffed. "It's a pity Tabitha sat him all the way at the other end of the table."

Murphy blinked. Did she think? Hank? "Oh, no," she spluttered. "I'm Tripp's girlfriend." The lie came easily but felt like mud on her tongue. Maybe she should have just let the lie go.

"He's in a coma. That's a shame as well." The queen dabbed at the corner of her mouth before placing her napkin in her lap and pushing her plate of half eaten salad away from her. A server came and whisked it away. Murphy's too, even though she wasn't really finished with it. Sighing she put her napkin in her lap and waited for the next course listening to the oh-hum conversations around her.

Did everyone think she was Hank's girlfriend instead of Tripp's? She glanced at Hank seated across the table and four people down. He was mid-laugh yet, as if her gaze was a magnet, looked over toward her. The candlelight from the table illuminated his face making his smile seem more magical. He lifted his hand in a wave. Murphy waved back and tried to suppress a laugh as Hank turned his hands into puppets and mimicked the old man next to him who while talking to him, was looking at his plate.

"Interesting." The queen muttered, an amused look gracing her wrinkles.

"What?" Murphy asked, moving her glass of water out of the way as a server placed a green looking bowl of soup in front of her.

"It just seems that my nephew fancies you."

"Your nephew?" The queen was Hank's aunt?

"Yes. I'm Richard Harrington's sister, Elizabeth." She pursed her lips. "Whatever that is good for."

Couldn't someone have warned her she was sitting next to family?

"Aunt?" she mouthed to Hank, hand shielding her from Aunt Elizabeth's gaze.

Hank shrugged, mouthing his apology.

"I guess I should have warned you about that one," Grandpa Jack chuckled, then loudly whispered. "Murphy, you're sitting next to Tripp's aunt."

"Thank you, Grandpa Jack," Murphy whispered back, doing her best not to roll her eyes.

"This soup is so great. Are you going to finish yours?" Grandpa Jack asked.

Murphy was still trying to catch up with the fact that she was sitting next to another member of the family and hadn't had a chance to even taste the soup going cold in front of her. "Sure, you can have it." She slid her bowl over, Grandpa Jack silently clapping in glee.

Murphy didn't miss Tabitha's look of disapproval. How she managed to witness the exchange from her place at the other end of the table was beyond Murphy. She bit the inside of her mouth. Was it just yesterday that she had hugged Murphy and told her that she was a breath of fresh air for the family? I guess that didn't include sharing soup at parties.

But Tabitha's disapproving glance wasn't what made Murphy's mouth feel like she had just sucked on cotton. The two girls sitting four seats down from Tabitha, sipping soup from a spoon, pinkies ridiculously extended, did. Charlotte Bane and Willow James — Claire's best friends. Her ladies in waiting. Her goons. How had she missed them before?

"Are you okay, Murphy? You kind of look like you've seen a ghost." Grandpa Jack chuckled, as the main course was whisked away.

Murphy nodded, moving her hands to her lap as a waiter placed a plate of sugary dessert in front of her. Creme Brûlée. One of her favorites, and she didn't even think she'd be able to stomach a bite.

CHAPTER EIGHTEEN

MURPHY HAD NEVER BEEN SO ready for a dinner to end. Every time one of the girls glanced her way, Murphy felt like she needed to dive for cover under the table. Of course, she didn't. She was sitting next to Aunt Elizabeth, and Tabitha was shooting her looks every five minutes. Or maybe those looks were for Grandpa Jack, but either way, she didn't hide under the table.

After lingering over the cream brûlée, Richard had tapped on his glass, toasted the success of his wife on another spectacular party, and asked everyone to join them in the ball room for dancing. Not that Murphy was looking forward to dancing, but she figured she could use her powers of being a wallflower to make sure she side-stepped Willow and Charlotte for as long as she could. Even with all the glances they shot her, if they recognized her, the news would already be out. Their network could put social media to shame.

Grandpa Jack escorted her to the ball room, laughing when he caught a glimpse of her bare feet and she told him Hank had stolen her shoes.

"Dad, seriously you sound like a buffoon." Tabitha hissed from behind them. Which only made him laugh harder. Richard pulled Tabitha away before she made too much of a scene.

"Was that a dinner or what?" Hank, escorting Eloise, sidled up next to Grandpa Jack and Murphy.

"That creme brûlée was to die for. Don't you think, Murphy?"

Murphy opened her mouth to answer, but was cut off by Grandpa Jack.

"The soup was my favorite. Hank, do you think you could get that recipe from Mrs. George for me before I go home?"

"Sure thing, Grandpa Jack. Are we ready to dance?" Hank held his hand out to Murphy. Her stomach flip flopped.

"Oh, no. I've already claimed this beauty's first dance," Grandpa Jack interjected, grabbing her hand and putting it in the crook of his elbow.

Murphy turned to Hank, apologetic, but not really. She wasn't sure her nerves could handle dancing with him.

"Besides, you promised me a dance." Eloise tugged on his arm. "Hank, you can't let me be on the sidelines. I'd die of embarrassment!"

The band had started playing an upbeat Christmas medley. Hank shrugged and allowed his sister to lead him to the dance floor. Surely that wasn't a look of disappointment Murphy had seen.

Grandpa Jack dropped Murphy's arm and offered his hand, bowing at the waist. "Shall we dance?"

Smiling, Murphy took his hand and followed him onto the floor. Four songs later they collapsed in comfy oversized chairs in a corner. Hank wandered off to find them all drinks. Grandpa Jack went in search of a snack declaring that, after all that dancing, he was hungry again.

"Are you having a good time?" Eloise asked, plopping down in the seat next to Murphy.

"I am. This is fun."

Eloise squinted her eyes at Murphy. "I'm so glad. I know you have to wish that Tripp was here."

"Where is Hank with those drinks? I'm parched." Murphy deflected Eloise's statement relieved when the younger girl turned to scan the crowd for her brother. It was on the tip of her tongue to tell her the muddled story of saving Tripp and meeting the family, but she reminded herself that wasn't what tonight was about. Tonight was just about having fun.

The band kicked it up a notch with a peppy pop song. Eloise squealed. "Murph, you'd better get very un-tired right now." Search forgotten, she stood up and grabbed Murphy's wrist pulling her to her feet. "You are totally dancing with me to this song. Right now."

The girls passed a baffled Hank balancing four glasses of ice water. Murphy shrugged when he asked where they were going, allowing herself to be pulled along. No thinking. Just doing.

Eloise led her out to the middle of the dance floor. She wasn't sure what she was supposed to do, but Eloise had her hands above her head and was singing at the top her of lungs to the song. Without looking around to see if anyone was paying attention to them or if anyone cared, Murphy joined in. She danced as if no one was watching.

The band played off the girl's energy and the next five songs were upbeat. Murphy danced until she felt like she was going to burst. She leaned over to Eloise to let her know that she was going to go to the bathroom. Eloise never opened her eyes or stopped swaying, just held two thumbs up in Murphy's general direction.

Murphy pushed through crowds of people, proud to say that she actually remembered where the downstairs bathroom (one of six?) was. She found this bathroom particularly weird since it had stalls. In a house. Who had bathroom stalls in a house? Murphy supposed it was because of so many parties held at the Harrington house over the years, but she still found it a little strange. She did however love this bathroom because in the middle there was a circular couch—or fainting couch or whatever rich people called them.

Murphy went to the bathroom, somehow holding her dress over her head to keep the back from dropping into the toilet and washed her hands. She pumped the Harrington rose lotion that was sitting on the counter into her hands. Sinking down into the circular couch, she relished in the quiet. Her ears were still ringing from the band—amazing as it was. She leaned her head back and let her eyes slid closed. She resolved to have fun and just enjoy being on the inside, so why was she not feeling it?

"But did you see that one girl?"

Murphy froze as two people walked into the bathroom. Who were they talking about?

"Oh my gosh. Yes. She's supposedly Tripp's brother's girlfriend, but what in the actual heck, where did he dig her up from?"

Murphy held her breath. Willow and Charlotte hadn't recognized her then, and once again she was mistaken for Hank's girlfriend.

"Her dress is so basic. I don't even think it's designer." They had made it to the mirrors now. One look behind them and they would have seen Murphy sitting there, shock written all over her face. She moved slowly around the couch. Not trusting that close up, in full light, she wouldn't be recognized.

Charlotte smoothed lipstick over her bottom lip and smacked both lips together. "I know right? And she's bare foot. Can you believe that? What does she think this is? A backyard shindig?"

Murphy slipped her exposed feet back under the hem of her dress as if that would deny the fact that her feet were bare.

"She hasn't even been dancing with Hank. Just that old man and duppy girl. With a man like Hank, I wouldn't let him out of my sight."

Charlotte shrugged. "Her loss. If I have my way, he'll be mine before the end of the night. Daddy said his trust fund alone could set a girl for life."

Murphy could feel the red rising in her own face. Her fingers curling into fists. Who did she think she was? Hank was more than just a consolation prize.

Willow tucked an imaginary hair back into place. "Did you catch her name? She doesn't go to Iverson, does she?"

If Murphy hadn't already been holding her breath she would have now.

"I don't think so, and there's no way she's at Iverson. Too bad Tripp's in a coma or we could have both brothers. Claire's loss."

Her lungs started to burn. Maybe there was a plus side to being so invisible at school. She had been at Iverson for seven years and yet they still didn't know who she was. This was who she wanted to be? A flimsy girl who's only goal in life was to get hot guy with a big pay out. One who didn't care if she hurt her best friend in the process of social ladder climbing. Murphy felt an ache behind her breastbone. That couldn't be her.

The girls finished their primping and stuffed everything back into their tiny wristlets.

"Let's go. Operation bag Hank Harrington commencing." Both girls giggled their way out of the bathroom never even seeing Murphy huddling on the couch.

She couldn't move. For years she had put up with backhanded comments from the elite at Iverson, but it took two minutes in a bathroom listening to Charlotte and Willow to make her realize she didn't really want to fit in at all. Not if it meant she had to be like that.

Sounds of the party crescendoed and faded again with the opening and closing of the door. The room felt like it was folding in on top of her. She had to get out of there. Grabbing her bag, she slipped it back on her wrist and headed out of the bathroom. Instead of going back to the party, Murphy turned toward the outdoor balcony. She needed air.

Cold air raced through her lungs, but she gulped it in anyways. The icy ground felt like it was shooting needles up her legs, but it was a welcome comfort, dulling the disappointment inside. She sagged against the balcony railing. Why had she really wanted to play this part? She did not fit in this crowd, nor did she really want to anymore. She was done. Emmaline had told her not to do anything rash at the party. To play the part. But she couldn't take anymore. She pulled her phone out of bag. Even though she'd have to give it back tomorrow, tonight it was her saving grace.

"There you are." Hank walked toward her, hands in his pockets, Murphy's heart beating fast with each step that brought him closer to her. "What are you doing out here?"

Murphy dropped her phone back into her bag and

turned to lean against railing. "I just needed some air, I guess."

"I totally get that," Hank blew out a breath. They were both silent watching it dance in mid-air before disappearing.

He leaned over the railing next to her, their shoulders practically touching. Did she really want to give this up? To give Hank up?

Tripp's girl. Tripp's girl. You want to be Tripp's girl. Pounded through her head. She and Hank would never work out. Could never be. She knew this with every fiber of her being.

"By the way," Hank turned, one hip still leaning against the balcony. "I had a talk with my dad this morning."

"Yeah?" She was doing her best to ignore the pounding of her heart and the Jiminiy Cricket stuck in her head. She clenched her teeth together to keep them from chattering. Maybe escaping to the balcony with no coat and no shoes in freezing temperatures hadn't been the best of ideas.

"Yeah. He agreed to let me switch my career path to music."

Murphy's heart shoved against her chest. "Hank, that's wonderful!"

"Well," Hank bumped her shoulder with his. "I owe it all to you."

"No, you don't." Murphy wasn't going to let him give her all the credit. "You had it in you the whole time. You just needed," she shivered, crossed her arms. "Needed a little point in the right direction."

"Oh, hey, you're cold."

Before she could protest, Hank had slipped his jacket off and pulled it over her shoulders.

Her feet, frozen numb, stumbled forward when Hank

tugged the jacket closed. She stopped herself from falling with two hands on Hank's solid chest.

"Why d-do I always s-seem to f-fall around y-you?" Murphy chattered out. "I p-promise I'm n-not this cl-clumsy."

Hank wasn't saying anything. Murphy fell silent feeling the rise and fall of his breathing. She stared at the perfect row of buttons on his shirt. Knowing that if she looked up, if she looked at Hank, it would be over. Everything would change, and there'd be no going back.

"Murphy." His voice was barely above a whisper shooting chills up and down Murphy's back.

She bit the inside of her lip acutely aware her hands were still pressed against him. She swallowed. The tingle down her spine had nothing to do with the cold anymore. Slowly she lifted her head. Hank's eyes were blue, but in the dim light they looked almost black. What she saw reflected in his eyes stopped her. Passion. Desire. Questions. She couldn't look away even though she knew what was coming. His gaze was a magnet drawing her closer. She should stop him. Needed to stop him. Kissing him was the point of no return. Her head tried to remind her she was supposed to be with Tripp. Her head was telling her this was all wrong. But her heart, with every beat, was screaming Hank's name.

Hank's hands rose, light as a feather framing her face. Heat radiated more sparks up and down every part of her. He leaned in. Noses brushing now. Murphy slid her eyes closed. This shouldn't be happening. This couldn't happen, but oh how she wanted it to happen. She wrapped her arms around Hank pulling him just a little closer.

"Hank, baby! Here you are."

Murphy pulled away as if she had been electrocuted.

Hank's gaze was pleading, wanting to draw her back in. She took a step back. What had she been about to do?

"Cain," Hank took a step toward her. Murphy put a hand up keeping him in place. She felt woozy.

Charlotte sidled up to him, wrapping herself around one of his arms. Murphy sunk into the shadows, stomach churning.

She turned and fled back into the house, dialing Lloyd's number as she went. Without remembering how, she made it to the front hall. She slipped out of Hank's jacket and handed it to a surprised looking Jarvis.

"This may be overstepping my bounds, but are you okay, Miss Cain?" Jarvis asked laying the wrap across Murphy's shoulders.

Murphy gave Jarvis a sad smile. She'd miss him. "I'm okay, Jarvis. Just ready to go home."

"Do I need to find Master Hank?"

"No," Murphy's voice caught, she had to force down the tears before continuing. "I have a ride coming to pick me up." A horn sounded from outside. "That would be it."

Jarvis opened the door for her, frowning slightly catching a glimpse of her bare feet. Still he escorted her down to the car, seeing her safely inside.

Murphy watched as Jarvis headed back inside, turning at the top step and waving. Murphy lifted her hand in a wave. Lloyd handed her a wool blanket from the back seat, mumbling something about the heater not working that great.

"Are you ok, Murph?" Floyd was staring hard at her.

"I am, Floyd. Just please take me home." Murphy blinked, hoping the car was too dark for him to see the tears swimming in her eyes.

"Murph, if we need to go rough up that Harring—"

"Please," Murphy cut him off. "I just want to go home."

Floyd studied her for a minute more before putting the car into gear and heading back to Iverson.

Thoughts of Hank whirled through her head leaving her lightheaded and heartsick. She vaguely thought her night had ended way too close to Cinderella's, shoes and all. She really hated that fairy tale.

TEXT NOTIFICATIONS

From Eloise Harrington (01:34 AM)

What happened to you tonight? I couldn't find you!

From Eloise Harrington (01:35 AM)

Hello?

From Eloise Harrington (01:47 AM)

Oooh it's late. I bet you're sleeping. Hope I didn't wake you!! Sorry!

CHAPTER NINETEEN

"I THINK I'M IN LOVE."

Murphy had closed herself in her room once they reached home. The twins, to give them credit, didn't follow or press her for answers. She only hoped they wouldn't return to the Harrington house and give Hank a piece of their mind for whatever they thought happened. The second she finished changing out of her dress, she video called Emmaline knowing that she'd be up waiting for all the details.

"Hello, to you, too. I had a great day, thanks for asking. Glad you had a wonderful time at the party, and that your neighborhood friendly fairy godmother made all your dreams come true. So, you think you're in love with a half dead guy? How does that happen?"

Murphy shook her head, eyes swimming. She knew she looked a mess. She ran a finger under her eyes trying to smear away the mascara, knowing it was already a lost cause. She hoped Emmaline couldn't see the dress in a heap where she had left it after her quick change into her holey sweats and old Yale t-shirt.

"If not with Tripp, then ..." Emmaline trailed off. She smiled sadly, her voice kinder when she figured it out. "Hank? I knew you were falling for him."

"I didn't mean to, Ems, it just kind of happened."

"Isn't that how all the good love stories happen?"

"Ems, he's so kind and funny. He's always taking care of his little sister. It's sweet, but there can't be anything there." Murphy twisted her hair up into a knot on top her head.

"Why not?"

Murphy rolled her eyes, forcing out a laughed around her sobs. "Because I'm not even in the same class as he his. I scrub toilets. Clean his brother's room. I'm always making a mess of things—look at the past two weeks!"

"You're just going to have to tell them the entire story, Murphy."

Murphy's stomach dropped. She knew that was going to be her only choice. "I can't."

"Why not?"

"What if they hate me?" She finally pinpointed why she couldn't ever get the words out. The realization made her cry harder.

"But what if they don't? Hank sounds like a really great guy. Maybe you should just give him a chance."

Murphy pressed her lips together. Swiped at the tears and snot running down her face. Just thinking about Hank made her chest tighten. The thought of telling him the truth and the disappointment she knew would come — she wouldn't be able to take it. Murphy would once again be the sad little orphan girl to be pitied. She'd rather not say anything and just fade away. That way she'd have a good memory. She'd *be* a good memory. "Even if he did forgive me, I don't belong in that world. Tonight was a *complete* disaster. I can't do that to him."

"That is just a bunch of bull—"

"Just leave it, Ems."

"Murph, you're breaking my heart." Emmaline looked like she was crying now too.

Murphy relished the ache behind her ribs. This is what she deserved. She had done this to herself. Mind spiraling it landed on Hank. Hank who smelled of cinnamon and sunshine. Who could make the piano sing with his long-tapered fingers. Who's smile could defuse unease almost instantly. Something in Murphy stirred when she thought of their almost kiss. The way he held her. That meant he felt something too, right? Maybe he was warring inside just as much as she was.

But why would he think of her that way? She could offer him nothing but scandal. She didn't come from money. She was awkward. Apparently more fit for "backyard shindigs" than parties and galas.

No. It would never in a million years work. Even if they both wished it. And the sooner her heart caught up with her head the sooner she could stop feeling like someone punched her in the gut.

———

MURPHY PULLED IN A DEEP, icy breath letting the cold air burn her lungs. It felt so good to run — and it had been at least three weeks since her last run. She could feel the stiffness in her muscles. Seven miles probably was too much to jump back into.

She looped around the park and headed back toward Iverson. Had it been just last week Hank taught her to drive here?

For a split second she thought about changing her route,

head to the Harrington House. Her thoughts echoed with the pounding of her feet.

Tell him. Tell him. Tell him.

Last night, after her chat with Emmaline, she'd resolved to disappear from the Harrington's lives, for real this time. It would be less painful for everyone that way. Still she wrestled with her decision. What if Emmaline was right about the Harrington's—Hank—forgiving her? Should she give them the chance?

She ran faster. Trying to outrun the thoughts ping ponging in her brain. She couldn't tell Hank. If he hated her, she would never be able to forgive herself. Wasn't having good memories with no goodbyes better than shattered hearts?

Murphy had totally and completely fallen for Hank. How could that have happened? She had been crushing on Tripp for as long as she could remember.

She should tell Hank—the entire story. It was *Hank*. He would understand. But if he didn't ....

Murphy felt like pulling out her hair. There was no way she and Hank would ever work. Tripp was eventually going to wake up, and everyone would see her the way she was. A nobody. They could never accept her. She was not of the Harrington's world, she was pretty sure the train wreck that was last night confirmed that even more. Each heartbeat and footfall pounded that truth into Murphy's thoughts.

The phone in her pocket vibrated. Lloyd. She sent it to voice mail, the past two weeks settling like a rock on her chest.

Tears burned the back of her eyes — more than just from the pain of the run. Why did she have to find herself in this situation? Why did she have to meet Hank at all? She should never have waited at the hospital.

Feeling like smoke was slowly filling her lungs, she stopped running. Bending over, hands on her knees, she sucked in frozen air. She choked in a sob and swiped a hand over her face smearing snot and tears all over the sleeve of her sweatshirt.

"Murphy?"

Murphy's breath hitched. Hank. She didn't even hear him drive up. His voice restarted the ache in her midsection. Why him? Why now? Maybe she should pretend that she didn't hear him. Keep running. Murphy picked her pace back up. Praying that he would get the hint, get back in his car and drive away. He didn't.

"Cain, wait up!"

It didn't take Hank long to catch up with her. He hadn't been running at a ridiculous pace for seven miles. He grabbed her elbow and turned her toward him. If she was running any faster, she would have splatted on the pavement. Murphy hung her head, trying to keep Hank from seeing the tears flowing down her face.

Hank bent, eyes searching for hers. "Murphy?"

She glanced at him through watery eyes. Confusion painting every corner of his face.

"Hey, hey, hey. What's going on?" Using his thumbs, he wiped at Murphy's tears. She tried to smile at him, to show him she was fine, but she just started crying harder. Why did he have to be so wonderful?

"Come here." Hank pulled Murphy to him. She inhaled the spice and citrus smell lingering on his coat, letting it warm her if only for a minute. Hank trapped her to his chest with his arms encircled around her back, his chin resting on her head. "Is this about last night? Listen. I'm really sorry about that. It was inappropriate," he growled frustration. "I'm not like that. I don't go after another man's girl, but I've never been so envious of my brother. That doesn't excuse my behavior, no matter how much I like you," Hank blew out a hot breath. "I promise I will be the perfect gentleman. You don't have to worry about me trying to put any moves on you. When Tripp wakes up, I'll step into the background and I won't get in the way."

His words came out like one big run on sentence, but Murphy could only concentrate on the part about him being envious of his brother. About *him* liking *her*. Emotions pressed in the space behind her breastbone. She shook her head, fingers gripping his stupid puffy jacket. If he knew who she really was he wouldn't have those same feelings.

"Tripp will pull through. He's a fighter."

The fact that Hank thought she was crying over whether or not Tripp was going to wake up made her cry even harder. She didn't care about Tripp that way—she wanted to scream.

Hank's lips brushed Murphy's head, and her heart almost stopped beating.

"Oh, Murphy," Hank whispered against her forehead.

What was Hank doing to her? She was a muddled mess.

"Come on," he sighed. "I'll drive you home."

Hank led her to his car and helped her to the front seat. She curled up, her back to the driver's seat. She was afraid if she looked at him, she would break. Maybe things would be different after she graduated. She'd be traveling the world, seeing places. She would be a different person, not the poor little, orphan girl that scrubbed gum off the walls. If she could keep up the façade for just a little longer, Hank wouldn't have to know who she really was, and maybe ... She scoffed. Who was she kidding? There wasn't going to be any travel. There would never be a her and Hank—she had promised. Last night was the last time. She knew she would always be that poor little nobody. She'd end up working at McDonald's and living in crummy housing on the wrong side of the tracks. She'd never be more than who she was. She pressed the heels of her hands into her eyes trying to pull herself together.

Hank jogged around the front of the car. A blast of cold air hit Murphy's back as he climbed in behind her, followed by a blast of hot air as he cranked up the heater, sitting for a minute to let Murphy's limbs thaw. She hadn't realized how cold she actually was.

Hank rubbed Murphy's back, and his hand stayed there as he drove the cold roads toward Iverson. If felt as if he was burning a hole in through her. Murphy bit her lip. This was crazy. She had three minutes tops before they arrived back at Iverson. She could tell Hank. She needed to get this weight off. Let the chips fall where they may. Nothing could be worse than what she was feeling now.

She sat up, turning in her seat. "Hank, I need to tell you—"

Her confession was cut off by the high twill of Hank's cell phone. Hank reached in his pocket and silenced it without looking to see who was calling.

He shook his head and looked over to Murphy, eyes imploring her to continue.

Murphy picked at a hangnail. She hated the habit, but she couldn't bear to look back at Hank. If she did, she'd lose her nerve.

Hank reached over and found her hand with his.

"Cain, whatever it is that's bothering you, you can tell me."

She hated the hot tears slipping silently down her face. She squeezed her eyes shut.

"That day at the train station—" Murphy started again.

The cell phone twilled again.

"Maybe you should answer that." Murphy suggested when Hank reached to silence it again.

He let the phone ring for two more breaths before answering it with a deep sigh.

Murphy's pocket dinged, and she pulled her cell phone from her pocket. She stared at the words Eloise had sent. She was going to be sick.

Hank's phone call lasted less than thirty-seconds. He ended the call with a whoop, letting his cell phone drop in the cupholder. "He's awake, Cain! He's awake."

TEXT NOTIFICATIONS

From Floyd Taylor (08:32 AM)

Call me! 911!!

From Eloise Harrington (08:42 AM)

Murphy! Tripp woke up! Where are you at? Get over here!!!

CHAPTER TWENTY

HANK PULLED A U-TURN, speeding toward home, taking half the time to arrive.

He's awake. Two of the most terrifying and relieving words that existed. Now that Tripp was awake, her secret would be revealed. She could go back to — to what? What exactly did she have to go back to? Peeling gum from the walls? Scrubbing toilets? That really wasn't a life. But it wouldn't be this fantasy life she had been living. Even if the fantasy was so nice.

Hank pulled up to the Harrington house with a screeching of breaks. Somehow, he had parked the car and was half out before it was even at a full stop.

Murphy followed at a slightly slower pace. She glanced over the space that separated Iverson and the Harrington house. She could see the smoke curling in the sky from Iverson. She snapped her sneakered feet together. If her shins weren't throbbing so much from her morning run, she could just jog back to Iverson, disappear from the Harrington's forever like she'd planned. They would quickly find out who she really was.

The thought of taking the easy-way-out made her sick to her stomach and turned her feet to bricks. Hank would come looking for her. Maybe she could bribe the twins to cover for her. It's not like Hank would be able to find her. He wouldn't think to look in the kitchen.

The twins—what had Floyd's message meant?

The Harringtons needed this family moment. She was just an outsider. Maybe it would be better if she wasn't here. Then she wouldn't see the hurt and betrayal in everyone's—in Hank's—eyes when they figured out the truth.

"Cain, you coming?" Hank reappeared at the open doorway, the hopeful look in his eyes chasing thoughts of escape from her mind.

Against her better judgement, she took the steps to the house two at a time, biting back the curse from her tired legs. The Harringtons had to have the truth from her. Not some pieced together guesses from confusion. They needed an explanation. She owed them that much. The ever-faithful Jarvis bowed to her, closing the door behind her.

She offered him a sad smile. This would probably go quick. As soon as she rounded the corner into Tripp's room, he'd know. This would be the last time she would be greeted by Jarvis.

She turned on her heel and threw her arms around the very shocked butler. "Thanks for everything."

The butler awkwardly patted her in the back. "Miss Cain?"

He smelled of peppermint and cloves. She had never noticed that before. "I know you don't understand, but really. Thanks. You are the world's best butler. You should have a mug with that on it. Do you have a mug? You should have a mug." Murphy pushed away, taking in his complete shocked expression. "Yes, well." She brushed at some non-existent crumbs on his shoulder. "Thanks."

"He's awake." Jarvis stated, face the color of the ribbon on the Christmas wreaths. "And, Miss—"

"I know," she turned and headed down the hall.

The door was open, light from the windows inside streaming into the hallway. She paused right outside the door. When she stepped across that line, everything was going to change. She wiped under her eyes with freezing fingertips. Pulling her sleeves over her hands, she scrubbed her face. Everything was changing whether she was ready for it or not.

The high-pitched laugh bubbling from out of the room made Murphy's blood turn to ice.

"Oh, yes, Fiji is just wonderful at this time of year, but when I heard what had happened to my Trippy Woo, I had to come be by his side."

Rounding the corner, Murphy saw Claire practically draped over Tripp, one hand tangled in his hair. Tripp, propped up on at least fourteen pillows, winced as a nurse pulled tape from whatever tube had been connected to his arm. Another nurse scribbled furiously on a clipboard.

Tripp looked good for a guy just waking up from a ten-day nap. A little pale, but otherwise good. All things considering. He had one hand rested on Claire's hip, thumb rubbing back and forth. Their PDA had never made Murphy sick before, but now, knowing what Claire had been up to, knowing it was all just a game to her, she wanted to throw up.

"What are *you* doing here?" Claire asked as if Murphy was a rotting piece of meat.

Richard and Tabitha, conversing with the Doctor, looked up at Clair's outburst. Grandpa Jack and Eloise, with matching uncomfortable smiles pasted on their faces, looked from Tripp and Claire to Murphy and back. Their looks asking Murphy to save them from the joke that was currently wrapped around Tripp. If only she could.

"M-Murphy is Tripp's girlfriend." Eloise stammered out an explanation.

Bless Eloise for defending her. Even with the evidence of her lie quite literally smacking them in the face.

Claire's laugh was ear piercing. Murphy almost forgot how annoying it could be.

"That's rich." Claire pointed an excusatory finger toward Murphy. "This is who you thought was Trippy's girlfriend?" Claire looked to Tripp's family as if it was obvious Murphy could never be one of them. "Murphy is nothing but a charity case. She's a nobody."

"Claire—" Tripp started before she stopped him with a sloppy kiss. Murphy could feel herself blushing. Her eyes darted to Hank and down to the floor. She shouldn't have looked at Hank frozen at the end of his brother's bed, a look of disgust painting his face.

Mrs. Harrington, mimosa clutched in her grasp like a lifeline, gasped. Eloise's teeth were biting her bottom lip. She looked like she was forcing herself to stay glued to her spot. Mr. Harrington standing behind his wife, hands in pockets. The nurses and Doctor were the only one to ignore the blatant affection of the two teens.

"Murphy," Mrs. Harrington finally took a sip—a long sip—from her flute. "This is ... Claire." Introducing her as if she didn't know what else to say.

Murphy felt herself nodding. Her mouth completely dry.

"I'm sure this is just a big misunderstanding. Murphy can tell us what is going on," Grandpa Jack pipped up. He was the only one who looked at ease lounging in the same chair Murphy had found him in most of the past week.

Claire put both arms around Tripp's neck pulling him closer. He looked as if he'd rather be strangled, but to give him credit, he didn't push her away. If looks could kill, the glare Claire was shooting Murphy would have her six feet under covered in worms and maggots.

"I..." Murphy wished she were six feet under. The worms and maggots would be preferable to the mess she had made herself. Her chest felt tight. "I'm sorry. I never meant—"

"Never meant what, Murphy?" Claire untangled herself and stood up, tugging her barely there skirt down. She planted her feet and crossed her arms. It was almost like she was protecting the family. More like the family needed protecting from Claire, but what could Murphy do? She was a nobody who didn't belong here.

Murphy took a deep breath. "I never meant for any of this to happen." She folded her arms, hugging herself. She shrugged. "After I saved Tripp at the train station, I rode up to the hospital and everything happened so fast. Hank thought that I was Tripp's girlfriend, and at the time, I wanted it to be true," Murphy stumbled over the admission. "And it was nice to...to belong. I didn't mean for it to go this far. I didn't think—"

Claire snorted. "Of course, you didn't think."

"You're right," Murphy was sick and tired of bowing to Claire's jabs and stabs. "I didn't think. I just did. I went with my gut. You were busy on your phone while Tripp ran back to get *your* purse. When he slipped and fell, *you* were still too busy to even notice that he'd been hurt. And instead of checking in on him, you just played with whatever Fiji Cabana boy was available."

Claire sucked in a breath, her face turning a scary shade of red.

Murphy didn't wait for her outburst before continuing. "I was so shocked when Hank thought I was Tripp's girlfriend, I didn't have time to correct him," she turned to face Tabitha and Robert. "I had every intention of telling you that morning of the brunch—"

"You've been eating here?" Claire squeaked.

"Hush," Tabitha Harrington hushed Claire, making everyone in the room jump. She turned back to Murphy, who took it as her cue to continue.

"But the brunch, while it was wonderful, sort of fell apart. And I started hanging out with Eloise and Hank and I've never had any of that before and didn't want it to end," she smiled at Eloise, and met Hank's eyes for the briefest of moments before quickly moving to Grandpa Jacks. "And I fell in love."

Grandpa Jack chuckled, "With me? Hot dog!" he slapped his leg causing everyone to burst out laughing. Except for Claire. She still looked like she was ready to murder Murphy.

"No. Yes!" Murphy waved an arm indicating the entire family. "Yes! All of you. You are all the best."

"I told you it was impossible for Tripp to have someone as wonderful as Murphy!" Robert exclaimed.

With his outburst, it seemed everyone started talking at once. All agreeing or disagreeing who it was who first figured out that Murphy couldn't be who she said she was. Murphy felt like a weight had been lifted from her shoulders. It didn't appear as if anyone hated her, but just the same, Claire was right in pointing out that she didn't belong here. She already knew that. She couldn't stay. She put the gifted cell phone on the nightstand table. She couldn't keep it.

Tripp caught her eye, before she disappeared out of the room and gave her a wave and half moon smile. She waved back, slightly sorry for the mess she had just left him, but Claire was curling back in his lap. He didn't look half so as accommodating after Murphy's Cabana boy comment.

She stepped into the hallway. She was invisible again.

Walking back to the front door, Murphy sucked in breaths to keep from losing it in the hallway. She wanted to sprint the rest of the way, but her legs still hurt from her run, dang it.

"Murphy! Murphy, wait!" Hank chased her up the hallway.

Murphy swiped her face. Commanded her tears not to fall. She stopped but didn't turn. She couldn't face him. She could feel him. He was so close. If she would just make herself turn. She slid her eyes closed. Took half a step back, her back pressing against his shoulder. His hands curling around her forearms.

"Murphy." Her name on his lips was a sigh and a question. She could hear the pain in his voice and it about broke her. "You could have told me." It was a whisper that she almost didn't hear.

"I tried so many times. I really did. And then," she shrugged. "I just couldn't. I couldn't bear it if you would hate me."

"I couldn't hate you."

She could feel the tears slipping. The relief that Hank didn't hate her radiating through her body. But she still didn't belong in his world.

"Stay," he pleaded. "Please. We'll figure this out."

She drew in a shaky breath, what was left of her shattered heart, breaking in two. If only it were so easy. If only she could step into the role. "I can't, Hank. You're you and I'm...me. I'd never belong here."

"Murphy—"

She turned and threw her arms around his middle, burying her face in his shirt. "Please, let me go."

His arm tightened around her, cheek resting on the top of her hair.

Her fingers gripped the back of his shirt. She wanted to always remember this moment. Hank's arms around her. His cheek on her head. His cinnamon sunshine scent. If she lingered, she would lose her nerve. She'd stay forever. She had to go. Now. She pulled away and almost ran the rest of the way to the door. She yanked it open, pulled it closed behind her. Ignoring the throbbing in her legs, she broke into a run. She had made it almost to the stone fence dividing the two properties before she realized that it was snowing.

A Murphy miracle.

Murphy felt it was more of a Murphy curse than miracle.

CHAPTER TWENTY-ONE

HEADMISTRESS KINGFISHER WAS BACK. Murphy knew as soon as she got back to Iverson. The air was tinged with commanded respect. Three students who had returned to school the day before scuttled by, books in hand. *Study* books. No one at Iverson studied during break. Unless there was a chance the Headmistress would find you. The smart kids locked themselves in their rooms.

Mistress Hyde of Iverson had cut her break short. She hadn't been due for another week. Nothing good could come from this.

"Hey, Murph, where have you been?" Lloyd bounded over to Murphy. If he noticed her splotchy, tear-stained face, he didn't mention it. He glanced over his shoulder as if waiting for The Hyde to step around the corner and give him three weeks detention, which, knowing Floyd and Lloyd, wasn't out of the scope of reality.

"I went for a run. Tripp woke up, and Claire already made it back to town, so yeah. Everyone knows." Murphy chewed on her bottom lip. She didn't want to stand here in the hallway chit-chatting. A long hot shower was calling her name. Not to mention the huge box of chocolates from Mr. Gruber. She planned on eating every single one of them while marathoning Doctor Who.

"Yeah, about that. Claire stopped by here before she went there. She had some kind of meeting with Kingfisher. Floyd and I tried to get her to tell us what the meeting was about, but she wouldn't." He stuck his hands in his back pockets. "I tried to call you on your phone, but you never answered. Now the Hyde is looking for you," Floyd looked over his shoulder again. "Murph, I think it's about Fiona. We tried to get into your room, but she wasn't there."

Murphy's stomach dropped. Could this day get any worse? She turned toward the Headmistress' office. Better just get this over with.

"Oh, and, Murph."

She swung back around.

"Happy birthday," Lloyd gave her two thumbs up before taking the stairs two at a time.

She was frozen. Birthday? It was December 27th already? This was taking the cake for most sucky birthdays.

"Miss Cain, can you please come in my office for a moment." Headmistress Kingfisher's voice seemed to float from her office.

Murphy pulled her hair out of its pony to quickly put it back up again. She swiped her face with the back of her sleeve, knowing she had to look like something the cat dragged in.

Squaring her shoulders, she faced the door. The best way for any meetings in the Headmistress' office was to get them over with quick like pulling off a bandage.

She was only a little surprised to see Mrs. Potts standing in the office as well. Mrs. Potts should have been gone for another two days. Murphy tried to swallow down a throat that felt like it was coated in cotton. Mrs. Potts looked angry. Her hands gripped the chair in front of her, knuckles white. Her face was beet red and eyes wild as she stared at a random object on the Headmistress' desk. Murphy tried to think back to a time she had seen Mrs. P angry and came up blank. She felt like her stomach was bottoming out. If this was Mrs. P's reaction, whatever it was, couldn't be good.

"Please, have a seat," Headmistress Kingfisher motioned to the seat in front of her desk next to the one Mrs. Potts had a death grip on.

Murphy side glanced at Mrs. P, who still hadn't looked her way, and back to the Headmistress. "I think I'll stand. Thanks."

Headmistress studied the two for a moment before lifting her shoulders in a shrug. "Whatever you wish."

Headmistress sat back in her chair and studied the duo in front of her, over her tortoise shelled glasses. She may not have been the tallest woman and may have been staring up at Murphy and Mrs. Potts, but there was no denying who had the power in the room.

Murphy glanced from Headmistress Kingfisher to Mrs. Potts and back, wishing someone would tell her what was going on already.

When Headmistress seemed to decide the stare down was over, she tented her hands together in front of her.

"Miss Cain," she drew out Murphy's last name more than necessary. "I've gotten some disturbing reports."

Disturbing reports? Who had given said reports? Claire? She hadn't been here for two weeks. Surely the Headmistress couldn't believe whatever Claire had claimed, could she? Was this about Fiona? Tripp?

When Murphy didn't say anything, she sighed and

continued. "It has been brought to my attention that you have been leaving campus the past couple of weeks."

Murphy felt like her lungs were forcing air through a straw. She didn't think leaving campus had been against the rules. And besides, she had had Mrs. Potts' permission. She glanced again at the older woman wishing that she would say something or look at her or *something. Anything.*

"And as such you have been failing on your duties here at Iverson."

She knew she maybe hadn't been doing her job to the fullest, but failing? She thought that might be taking it a bit far.

"Why is Mrs. Potts here?" Murphy asked in barely a whisper. Mrs. Potts shifted uncomfortably.

Headmistress turned to Mrs. Potts as if just realizing she was still standing there.

"Carol is here as she was the acting representative of Iverson."

Murphy could feel her fingers ball into fists, readying herself for whatever bad news came from the woman in front of her.

"With the travesty at the train station and how these past weeks have been handled, Carol Potts has been let go from Iverson due to her incompetence."

"What the—"

"Miss Cain!" Headmistress Kingfisher cut off Murphy's protesting, smoothing her jacket of non-existent wrinkles before continuing. "I would appreciate if you would refrain from such outbursts, and it would behoove you to watch your language."

Murphy took a breath, trying to calm her raging nerves. "There's no reason you need to fire Mrs. Potts." Mrs. Potts loved this job. What would she do now? This was all her fault. "Please. I take full blame for everything."

"Murphy," Mrs. Potts turned and put her hand on Murphy's arm. Murphy shrugged her off.

"You shouldn't lose your job because of my bad choices." She had to make Headmistress Kingfisher understand. She had to fix this.

"Be that as it may," the Headmistress cut in. "My decision is final. Carol, you may go." She dismissed Mrs. Potts.

Mrs. Potts looked as if leaving Murphy in the lion's den was the last thing she wanted to do, but Murphy pushed her toward the door wanting to get her out of the line of fire as much as possible. Mrs. Potts squeezed her hand before disappearing, closing the door behind her. The click echoed in the silence of the room. Murphy studied the towering bookshelf covered in books. She'd be surprised if Her Royal Highness had ever cracked any of the spines. She didn't strike Murphy as a reader. She stared at the intricate design in the dark crown molding. The swish and swirls in the Oriental rug beneath her feet. Anywhere except for at Headmistress Kingfisher.

"Miss Cain," the Headmistress' tone was ice. "Is it true that you have had a pet on school property?" Her thin eyebrows rose.

"I—"

Without breaking eye contact, Headmistress Kingfisher reached to something beside her, out of view from Murphy. She set an animal carrier on her desk. Fiona mewed. She was more than annoyed.

Murphy's heart sank. Apparently this day could get worse. She hung her head. "Yes, ma'am."

It'd be so easy to explain the Fiona situation, but that would mean throwing Tripp under the bus. If anything, she felt she owed Tripp and the Harringtons. She could give them this. It wasn't as if Headmistress Kingfisher would listen to her anyway. She could tell the Head-mistress' mind was made up. Fiona could have belonged to the President and it wouldn't have made any difference.

"You are aware of Iverson's policy on pets. Are you not?" It was statement, but Murphy answered anyway.

"Yes, ma'am."

Headmistress Kingfisher nodded. Looking slightly surprised. Did she want Murphy to agree with her? She had the evidence right there in a horrible purple colored cat carrier. Murphy was tired of lies. Was tired of the deception.

"You will gather your things."

Murphy's head snapped up. Gather her things? But didn't that mean? "You're kicking me out?"

Headmistress Kingfisher looked up from the paperwork she was tidying on her desk. "Miss Cain, you broke school policy. You admitted that you knew you did so. I see no other recourse than to dismiss you. You are now eighteen. Legally an adult."

Murphy blinked. "B-but where am I supposed to go?" She was supposed to have a little bit longer before she needed to figure it out.

The Headmistress heaved a sigh as if dealing with Murphy had taken a toll. "I don't know, nor do I care. I'm sure you will figure it out. I will let you have one day to gather your things and make preparations to leave. I will need you off the premises by noon tomorrow."

Murphy could see by the challenging stare in the head-mistress gaze that she excepted her to beg on hands and knees to stay. But Murphy just stood there, mute, watching the woman straighten her desk around the cat carrier that continued to growl and hiss at her.

Murphy didn't have any tears left to cry, and even if she did, she certainly wasn't going to give Mistress Kingfisher the satisfaction. She was completely ... numb.

Since she was leaving, there was one more question she had to ask. "Why do you hate me so much?"

Headmistress Kingfisher looked up in surprise. "Murphy, I don't hate you," her tone of voice said otherwise. "Someone has to teach you the hard lesson that life isn't easy."

Ironic since most of the students in her school weren't learning that life lesson in the least.

Murphy nodded. Stepping forward she curled her hand over the handle of the carrier lifting it off the desk. She could see the Hyde's mind was made up.

"Please do not let that thing out of the cage for the remainder of your stay."

Murphy didn't reply. She turned and walked out of the office letting the door slam shut behind her.

NOTIFICATION CENTER

Message from Emmaline Harris (08:42 AM)
HAPPY BIRTHDAY!!!!

CHAPTER TWENTY-TWO

IT WAS STILL SNOWING when Murphy woke up the next morning. Big fat flakes floated past her window.

Today was the day she was leaving Iverson. Her eyes and nose were raw, her throat felt like she had dined on sandpaper. *Not like this. I didn't want to leave like this.* Leaving was supposed to be on her own terms. It was supposed to involve a plan.

For the first time that she could ever remember she wanted to stay at Iverson. She was finally breaking free, and all she wanted to do was stay.

Her wall was now bare. Map carefully folded and squeezed in the slot next to her computer. Everything she owned fit into one suitcase, one duffle bag, and the satchel the twins had gotten her for Christmas—which were all stacked by the door.

Mrs. Potts had been waiting outside the door when Murphy stormed out of the Headmistress' office. They practically marched to the kitchen together, holding their heads high — not that anyone had been hanging around waiting for a verdict. Murphy had been glad that school wasn't back in full session yet. As it were, she'd be gone before everyone showed back up.

Murphy apologized again and again, but Mrs. Potts just shrugged her off. She had been planning on retiring after next year anyway. The visit with her daughter and grand-kids made her ache for a simpler life. She had already decided to move in with her daughter until she found a place of her own.

Murphy knew she could call Emmaline. She *should* call Emmaline, but she didn't want to feel like she was taking advantage of anyone anymore. Floyd and Lloyd stopped by while she stuffed clothes in a suitcase and helped her wiped everything down. They had put together what had happened through the school grapevine. It had been Willow and Charlotte that had turned her in to Claire. Head-mistress Kingfisher had come home early because a storm had cut her vacation short—nothing to do with Murphy.

Willow and Charlotte had put two and two together after Murphy left the party. Charlotte, after getting shut down numerous times from Hank, somehow had found out that everyone thought Murphy was *Tripp's* girlfriend. Willow saw Murphy get in the car with Floyd and Lloyd, and both girls decided to text Claire who had apparently already been stateside. After getting the full story, Claire had made a visit to the Headmistress. When they couldn't find Murphy that morning, Fiona was discovered in her room. Claire had to have arrived at the Harrington's only a few minutes before Hank and Murphy had gotten there.

Stretching in bed, Murphy smelled the air waiting for that first whiff of morning coffee, until she remembered that Mrs. Potts had already left to go back to her daughter's—after their failed plan making session the night before. Mrs. Potts wanted Murphy to stay with her at her daughter's house, but there was barely enough room for her as it was. Mr. Gruber offered Murphy his extra room, but since he still lived on campus, she declined his offer. She really didn't want someone else to get in trouble trying to help her out.

In the end, Mrs. Potts and Mr. Gruber had shoved some bills into her hand. Not much, but enough to get a hotel room for a few days and work on figuring out a game plan, find a job.

Murphy stared numbly at the white ceiling, listening to Fiona purr in her ear. She had completely ignored the Headmistress demand to keep the cat cooped up in the carrier. She wasn't happy being contained in the tiny space. It wasn't like the Headmistress could kick Murphy out of school again. Been there, done that.

Pushing back the covers, Murphy rolled out of bed, careful not to upset Fiona too much. Not even the chill in the room bothered her already freezing body.

Skipping a shower, she got ready, acutely aware of every "last-day-at-Iverson" task she was performing. How strange it was to think in lasts. She assumed this was what someone graduating and moving to the next stage in life would feel like. Minus the absolute despair from being kicked out early and the fear from the lack of a destination.

Dumping a cup of food into Fiona's dish, she shook her head and pasted on a smile. At least Fiona didn't seem to mind they were going on an adventure.

In search of food, Murphy wandered into the kitchen. Beth, the part time help who got a promotion with Mrs. P's vacancy, was already beginning to prep lunch with a new assistant. Murphy hated the pang she felt at being replaced so quickly. So easily.

"Breakfast in the mess hall has already been cleaned up," Beth said without turning from the counter.

Murphy stood in the middle of the kitchen. She wasn't sure if Beth would like if she got in the pantry or not. Mrs. Potts had never minded, but then again Mrs. Potts always saved her food when she slept in and had a fresh pot of coffee waiting. Murphy looked to where the coffee pot sat on the counter. Shiny, clean and very, *very* empty.

Ignoring Beth's voice droning on about what she should and shouldn't be doing per the Headmistress' orders, Murphy headed toward the back staircase. Maybe the twins would have an energy drink. She needed caffeine.

Heading up the stairs, she picked at the polish on her nails. Only two days ago this was a perfect manicure for the perfect evening. The Harrington Christmas Ball seemed forever ago. Murphy sucked in a deep breath. So maybe now, just a little bit, she wished she'd taken Hank up on his offer to stay. She could figure this out on her own. She had to. She'd stay a night in the inn and make a plan. Go from there.

When she'd watched Tripp fall, she never would have guessed she'd end up here.

Murphy knocked on the twin's door. There was no answer.

Strange.

She knocked again.

Peter Cho stuck his head out of his bedroom, smacking hard at a piece of gum. "They aren't here. Left to go somewhere this morning."

Murphy blinked. When had Peter gotten back to campus?

Surely the twins would be back before she had to go. "Did they say where they were going?"

"Somewhere." Peter shrugged a shoulder before disappearing back into his bedroom.

Murphy went back to picking at her polish. No point it trying to keep it perfect since it was already half gone. She turned on her heel. What now? There was at least another half hour before her taxi would arrive. Mr. Gruber wanted to take her to the train station, but the Headmistress had found something to keep him busy.

She huffed out a sigh and pushed her hair back from her face. There were a lot of decisions that she was going to have to make on her own in the next couple of days. Time to grow up. She sunk her hands into her hoodie, hoping to keep herself from chipping off all her polish. She guessed she could go ahead and move her bags and Fiona out to the hallway. Maybe she'd see the twins before she left and maybe she wouldn't. The thought made her ache. It was bad enough that she wasn't going to get to see Emmaline.

It took her a good fifteen minutes to get Fiona back into her carrier. She promised the cat that she wouldn't leave her there for long. She debated on taking the cat to the Harringtons. In the end, she figured that she'd contact Tripp later. Truth was she'd kind of gotten attached. She secretly hoped that he wouldn't, or couldn't, take her back.

Stacking the duffle bag on top of the suitcase, she slung the computer bag over her shoulder, and grabbed the cat carrier. Fiona let her know just how unhappy she was at her current situation with a strangled meow. Murphy hoped she'd calm down sooner rather than later.

Looking back into her now empty room, she felt a pull. The place that she called her own for the past seven years now looked like an empty shell. Murphy wondered if the Headmistress would let her replacement have this room.

She snorted. The Headmistress would most likely turn this into a second pantry. The school needed it.

Leaving her door open, she pulled the suitcase behind her listening to the click clack as the wheels bounced over tile. Fiona's mewing almost sounded like she was trying to make music.

No. Murphy tilted her head. There was actual music playing. She furrowed her brow. Was that—? It couldn't be.

Someone was playing Your Song. She followed the sound of Elton John's voice through Iverson and ended in the grand entryway. Murphy let the handle of her suitcase go and it fell to the floor with a clatter.

"It's you."

What was Hank doing here? Standing there in dark jeans, a hoodie, and the black Converses he was always wearing, he held out a cupcake with so much pink icing on top that it looked like it was getting ready to slide off. A single candle stabbed through the middle was flickering. She wanted to feel something other than the numbness. He remembered. The song, the cupcake. She had told him they wouldn't work. Why was he making this harder than it needed to be?

Murphy glanced over Hank's shoulder. Eloise was bouncing on her toes. The biggest smile Murphy had ever seen on the girl's face. Floyd and Lloyd, with their arms around each other looking like they were pulling off the biggest prank ever. And an elderly woman, tears glistening in her eyes. The woman looked vaguely familiar, but Murphy couldn't place her. "What are you doing here?"

Hank ignored her question, his smile faltering for half a second at the flatness of her tone, before lighting back up. "What's with the luggage, Cain? Are you going somewhere?"

Murphy looked down at the luggage at her feet. Fiona let out another annoyed meow. Almost as if telling Hank how observant he was.

She set Fiona down. The carrier got heavy fast. She toed the tile with her scuffed up converse, trying not to compare her old, worn-in pair with the newness of Hank's. She sighed not really wanting to re-tell the entire story, she shortened it. "I have been dismissed from Iverson, so I'm heading out."

"You what?" Hank took a step forward, but remembering the burning candle stopped. "What happened?"

Murphy squinted her eyes. "Why are you here?"

"Well, for starters, we missed your birthday." Hank looked back at Eloise who waved at Murphy. "Wheezy was just beside herself when we realized it was yesterday. So, we decided we would pop over and say happy birthday. Grandpa Jack is back at the house hoping you'll swing by for a game of cards later. He says to bring your pipe."

Murphy felt her head shaking back and forth. "But, yesterday—"

"What about it?"

"Hank." Murphy bit her lip. Was he really going to make her relive everything? Admit again how wrong she was.

"Murphy. I told you we could work it out."

She let out a shaky breath. Her name on his lips would forever send chills over her. "I lied, and I'm not like you. I don't come from money. I—" Her voice cracked. Of course, now the tears decided to start back up.

Hank put a finger to her mouth putting a stop to her self-sabotage. "If I recall correctly, you never actually said you were Tripp's girlfriend. That was actually me." He put his thumb to his chest. "Plus, you tried to tell me, probably multiple times, but I would never shut up and listen. I don't care that you aren't like me. That's one of the things I love so much about you. Also," he leaned forward and motioned Murphy to do the same.

He was infuriating. And wonderful. Murphy bent closer.

"I already knew your secret. Now can you blow out this candle before it slides off this cupcake and you don't have a candle to blow out?"

Murphy stopped breathing. He already knew? "H-how?"

He held the cupcake two inches from her face, eyebrows raised.

Murphy rolled her eyes and blew the candle out. The crowd behind Hank cheered. She rolled her eyes. "What do you mean you already knew my secret? How could you have known?"

Hank passed the cupcake back to Eloise. "I overheard you talking to Tripp, back when we brought him home. You weren't very quiet about it," he chuckled.

Murphy thought back. Tried to remember exactly which day it was that they had brought Tripp home, when she had poured her heart out to him. It had to have been the day she took Fiona for an early morning visit.

"All this time!" She punched Hank's arm. At least he had the decency to pretend that it hurt. "You knew all this time and you didn't say anything. Why didn't you say anything?"

Murphy wanted to kiss the smug smile off Hank's face. She also wanted to smack him.

"I figured you'd tell us when you needed to. Didn't seem like my place to out you. And besides you brought life back to the family. Mother and Grandpa Jack are actually talking again. And other than being completely scared by Claire, she seems to be changing. For the better."

"Claire scares everyone." Her comment was met by "hear-hear" from the twins.

"And, me, Cain. You changed me." Hank groaned and stepped forward, grabbing up both of her hands in his. He leaned forward and put his forehead to hers. "I never would have had the courage to talk to my dad about my music if you hadn't pushed me."

Murphy was shaking her head, woozy at the closeness of him. He was intoxicating. "That was all you."

"Don't," he said. "You helped more than you give yourself credit for."

"I love you." The admission slipped out before Murphy had a chance to think about what she was saying.

"Grandpa Jack is going to be so disappointed."

Murphy laughed.

"I love you too, Murphy Cain."

He closed the gap his lips landing on hers. The world melted away. She wasn't worried about what was coming next. This. Right here in this moment. She knew everything was going to work out. That she'd be ok. She pushed on her toes, deepening the kiss. Being this close to Hank reminded her of being wrapped in a warm blanket on a cold day with her favorite cup of cider.

She wrapped her arms around his middle and pulled him closer. Her toes tingled, and she loved it.

Slowly she remembered that they had an audience who was currently cheering and clapping bringing in the attention of others that were loitering the halls of Iverson.

She broke away breathless.

"Wow," Hank mumbled.

"Yeah," Murphy agreed.

"What is all this ruckus out here?" Headmistress King-fisher's presence caused the Iverson students to scramble. Murphy took a step back from Hank.

He immediately pulled her back to his side.

"Miss Cain, it's almost noon. I do expect you off the premises." She stopped when she realized there were outsiders standing in the hallway.

The older lady stepped forward.

"G-Gemma DuPonts."

Murphy looked back and forth between Headmistress Kingfisher and the older lady. Gemma DuPonts? Hearing that last name, it clicked. Her mother had been a DuPonts. There had been an old faded picture in her mother's things of two girls in party dresses and a tall boy behind them. The lady that stood before her was a little older and a little grayer, but this was definitely her mother's sister.

"Yes, Sonora." Gemma practically glided over the floors Murphy and Mrs. Potts had polished the week before. "I find it strange that I was never contacted about my niece after my mother's passing."

The Headmistress put a hand to her chest. Stammering through an explanation. "But I figured the courts would have. I never dreamed that you wanted this child—"

"This child," Gemma pointed to Murphy. Her features softening. "This child was my sister's daughter. My mother only lived two weeks after finding out about Murphy, and both my brother and I had been out of the country." She stepped over and grasped Murphy's hand. "She said she had an important matter to discuss with us once we were back stateside, but she passed before getting a chance to explain."

She turned to Murphy. Hank stepped to the side letting Murphy and Gemma have a moment to themselves.

"Please, please, forgive me. We had no idea Corine had a daughter. I could hardly believe it myself when Hank phoned. I thought it was all just a joke. But this one," she motioned with her chin to Hank. "He can be quite persuasive. Can you ever forgive me?"

Headmistress Kingfisher let out a snort. "This is so rich."

Gemma turned on one high heel, and the fact that she didn't even teeter made Murphy like her already. She slowly walked until she stood in front of Sonora. "Excuse me?"

"I—"

"No," Gemma cut her off. The twins started laughing at the Headmistress' squirming, but Gemma stopped them with a look. "You don't get to make any excuses. I knew you didn't like me when we went to school, and you made it pretty clear you weren't a fan of our family. I never understood it, tried to be nice to you. But you've taken it too far. To treat one of your students—my niece or not—like a servant? And to not even reach out to family when you knew you had connection? That is taking it too far."

"The courts put her under my care. I was to raise her as I saw fit." Sonora spluttered another excuse, clasping her hands in front of her, as if shielding her from Gemma's onslaught.

Gemma's eyes narrowed. "The courts will be hearing of what you see as 'fit.' I don't believe *servitude* is what they had in mind."

Cheers erupted from the twins and they high fived each other as Gemma returned to Murphy's side. The Headmistress slammed her foot down like a spoiled child and stomped off to her office, slamming the door behind her.

Gemma was doing her best to keep a straight face, but

Murphy could see a smile playing at her aunt's mouth. Murphy didn't know what she was feeling. She was floored. This woman, her *aunt*, just stormed in here and put Head-mistress Kingfisher in her place and barely batted an eyelash. She felt such pride.

The Grandfather clock in the hall chimed the hour at the same time a chime went off on someone's phone.

Lloyd cleared his throat. "Um, Murph? Your taxi's here."

"I wished our first meeting wasn't so rushed," Gemma said. She put her hands on Murphy's shoulders, her kind, gray eyes looking directly into hers. "Murphy, I want you to come live with me. If you want. I want to learn everything there is about you. Hank has filled me in on a little, but I want to know more. Would you like that?"

Murphy looked over to Floyd, Lloyd, and Eloise all looking as if they were barely able to keep their excitement contained. Hank stood with his hands in his pockets and a grin tugging at the corners of his mouth. Her problems—where to live, what to do, how she was going to make it—were all unfolding, fixing themselves in one big swoop. She already loved Gemma, her powerful strong, beautiful aunt. Aunt! Family. She had real family! She couldn't stop thinking it. Her face hurt from smiling so big.

Murphy felt herself nodding. She wanted nothing more to get to know her mother's family. "Yes."

Gemma clapped her hands together. "Lloyd was it? Or are you Floyd?" Both twins snapped to attention. "You can cancel that Uber. Let's get Marvin to get my nieces things in the car. We're getting out of this wretched school." She headed with the twins and Eloise to the front door, mumbling something about never really liking Iverson anyway.

Murphy turned to Hank. "So. You did all this?"

He shrugged, cheeks reddening. "Yeah, I guess so."

"How in the world?"

Hank settled his arm around her waist. "I googled you."

"You what?" Murphy lightly pushed away from Hank; eyebrow cocked.

"There was a little more to that," Hank admitted. "But you can really learn stuff about someone when you Google them. Anyways you said your dad was a professional piano player, and I was a little curious about how you ended up here. Did you know there had been a small write up in the newspaper about your dad's death, and it mentioned the court and your grandmother. At first, I just wanted to find her to figure out why she just left you in this place, and through digging I found out that she had actually passed not shortly after placing you here. One thing led to another, I found your aunt and here we are."

"You're amazing, Hank Harrington." Murphy reached up on her tippy toes give him a kiss. Kissing Hank was quickly becoming her favorite.

Fiona growled angrily.

"Were you stealing my brother's cat?" Hank picked up the hissing cat carrier, holding it away slightly away.

Murphy paused. "Well, I . . . I guess I was." She shrugged. "Headmistress was never going to let her stay, so really I rescued her."

Hank looked into the front of carrier. Fiona hissed and lunged at the door. "Eesh. She is not happy about being in this carrier. We may have to let her out in the car."

"We? Are you coming with me?" Murphy grabbed the handle of her suitcase and rolled it behind her.

"Of course I'm coming with you, Cain." He bopped her nose as he headed out the door to the waiting car.

"Sounds good to me." Murphy stopped at the door, turning to look back at the now empty halls of Iverson. The students having lost interest once Headmistress Kingfisher disappeared in her office.

She smiled. This hadn't had been the best of places for the last seven years, but being at Iverson had lead her to Hank and the Harringtons and her Aunt Gemma—her family. It made her realize she wouldn't have traded this time for anything.

In the years to come, when asked what her favorite memory was, she would always begin her story with it happened at Christmas.

ACKNOWLEDGMENTS

If you've made it this far it means you've finished (or if you're like me, it's the first thing you're reading, so hello!!).

To Andy. You're my best friend. My rock. My real-life hero. I love you so much. Thank you for supporting all my crazy ideas and dreams and doing this thing called life with me. You're the best. Forever.

To Elsie, Drew, and Oliver. You guys are my favorite humans ever! Thank you for getting excited about mommy's book (and not being angry that we had cereal *again* for dinner). You three are my everyday inspiration.

Emilie Haney. Girl. Seriously. Thank you for putting up with me and my thousand questions, millions of edits, and gazillion texts (seriously, there were a lot). Thank you for, hands-down, the best cover I could ask for (and thank you for sticking with me for my thousand and two little tweaks). All your help on the inside and outside of the book helped me make Murphy shine just a little brighter, and I will be forever grateful.

Nesya Walker. Thank you for going on this journey with me. For being my sounding board. Helping me unstick myself. And for writing Hank's Song. It's beautiful. You're amazing. (Now finish writing your dang book!)

Natalie Walters, thank you for helping me craft this story into existence. From jabbering about a little flash fiction story to a full-fledged novel (whoops). Also, thank you for Iverson Prep. I seriously suck and naming things and could never have come up with that one without you.

Linsay Adair, thank you for falling in love with Hank and Murphy and telling me to keep going when I wanted to trash it. For your eyes when I wasn't sure where to put commas and when I spelled words wrong, thank you for fixing them. You're the best.

Joelle Hirst and Gabrial Jones — my first readers. I love you both, and I'm so glad you loved this story, even though you were fairly certain I was going to kill everyone at the end.

Laurie Tomlinson, Grant Gardner, Kelsey Hendrix thanks for our water cooler chats and for all the encouragement. You keep me (mostly) sane. Also, there's a cameo of our favorite character in here — did you see him?

Mom and Dad, thank you for putting the love of books and words into me. I'm still trying to figure out what you did so I can pass it along to my kids. I love you always.

Anette, you are seriously the best mother-in-law a girl could ever ask for. I thank Jesus for you every single day. Thank you for taking the kids for weekends at a time so I would have long writing sessions.

Adam, Brandon, and Brittney —Y'all the best siblings ever. I'm glad I'm stuck with you. I love you forever and always.

Kacee Brown thank you for being my right-hand woman and second mama to my kiddos. For doing school pick up (and feeding them) when I was so far in edits I couldn't dig myself out.

(Also, Noah Brown — Happy stinkin' birthday, kid!)

And finally, to you, my readers (My readers! I'm still so tickled I get to say that!!). I'm so honored that you picked up my little book! Thank you for taking a chance on me and this little book. I will forever be grateful.

ABOUT THE AUTHOR

| Photo by Brittney Melton

Christen Krumm lives with her real-life superhero husband and three barefoot wildings in small-town Arkansas. Coffee is the lifeblood, books are her drugs, and creating stories is her favorite. Find her online at christenkrumm.com

twitter.com/christenkrumm

instagram.com/christenkrumm

Made in the USA
Middletown, DE
25 November 2019

79444856R00142